The Ten Per Cent Gang

I. J. PARNHAM

ROBERT HALE · LONDON

First published in Great Britain 2004

ISBN 0 7090 7573 1

Robert Hale Limited
Clerkenwell House
Clerkenwell Green
London EC1R 0HT

Typeset by
Derek Doyle & Associates, Liverpool.
Printed and bound in Great Britain by
Antony Rowe Limited, Wiltshire

The Ten Per Cent Gang

Sheriff Wes Creed has suffered yet another disastrous day. Earlier, Clayton Bell's bandit gang raided a cash shipment bound for Lincoln's bank. And while Creed fruitlessly pursued the bandits, the vigilante organization, the Ten Per Cent gang, calmly tracked and reclaimed the stolen cash. And for their trouble, the vigilantes retained their usual fee – ten per cent of the loot.

With the Ten Per Cent gang now threatening to enforce all justice in Lincoln, Creed realizes he has to slap them in jail, even if it means riding roughshod over every law in the land.

So Creed has no choice but to forge an alliance with the only man who hates the Ten Per Cent gang as much as he does – Clayton Bell.

By the same author

The Outlawed Deputy
The Last Rider from Hell
Death or Bounty
Bad Day in Dirtwood
Devine's Law
Yates's Dilemma

CHAPTER 1

The sheriff's third gunshot was even closer. The lead whistled by only scant feet from Fletcher Grange's right ear.

While gripping the reins tightly in one hand, Fletcher fired a speculative shot over his shoulder, then thrust his gun into his belt and hunched forward in the saddle.

Beside him, Hardy Newman glanced over his shoulder too.

Sheriff Wes Creed and Deputy Alan Fairborn *were* gaining on them.

Hardy spurred his horse to even greater speed, sending up huge plumes of dust in his headlong dash across the plains towards a huge mesa ahead.

'What you reckon?' Hardy shouted.

'They had a lot of time to make up,' Fletcher shouted back. 'Their horses are tired. We'll break them.'

Hardy nodded and concentrated on hard, fast riding.

As they swung around the mesa, Hardy glanced back and sure enough, the chasing lawmen were out of firing range, the last mile having taken its inevitable toll on their straining mounts.

Hardy and Fletcher allowed themselves a joyous whoop of delight and, by the time they swung out from the other side of the mesa, the following lawmen were slowing to a halt and they whooped some more.

Even so, for the next two miles, both men frequently glanced back, but the lawmen's pursuit had died.

With their last obstacle resolved, they swung off the trail and headed for a rocky uprising.

Closer to, a triangular tangle of gnarled trees appeared. Hardy and Fletcher pulled back on their reins and glanced around. They both saw the lines of hoof-prints leading towards the trees.

The two men glanced at each other and shared a nod. With Fletcher ten paces back, Hardy edged his horse towards the trees, his Colt pulled and ready.

'Where are the horses?' Hardy muttered.

Dave Gordon should have left fresh horses for them here.

Fletcher glanced at the hoof-prints, which led behind the trees. 'I reckon that idiot didn't tether them properly.'

'Then I'll teach him a lesson he won't forget.' Hardy clenched a fist beside his neck and mimed a noose tightening.

Fletcher grunted his agreement, then pointed at a

huge boulder to the right of the trees.

Hardy turned. He narrowed his eyes and edged his horse forward two more paces. From behind the boulder a horse's head swung into view.

A smile spread across Hardy's grim visage, then died.

The horse had a rider—just the toe of his boot was visible.

Hardy glanced back at Fletcher and mimed a knife slicing across his throat, then pointed at the boulder.

With slow stealth, Fletcher slipped from his horse, then dashed to the other side of the boulder. He pressed his back to the rough stone and slipped his gun from his belt.

'Is that you, Dave?' Hardy shouted, holding his gun at arm's length and aimed at the side of the boulder.

The horse edged the shortest of paces forward.

Hardy tightened his finger on the trigger.

Then hot fire punched into Hardy's shoulder, the rifle blast echoing a fraction later. As Hardy plummeted from his horse, Fletcher slammed back against the boulder, a gunshot blasting into his arm. His gun flew end over end before it crashed into the earth.

Hardy lay a moment, his shoulder numb, but his gun had landed two yards before him. He pressed his head to the ground, the harsh rock grinding into his forehead.

Then he leapt for the gun. Just as his left hand brushed the cold metal, a gunshot wheeled it away from him, a second shot spinning it far out of his reach.

With a desperate glance, he searched out Fletcher, but Fletcher had slid to the ground, nursing his arm and staring behind Hardy with his mouth open in silent shock.

From behind Hardy, steady footsteps approached, each step grating on Hardy's frazzled nerves. Hardy shuffled round and looked up to face a black-clad figure, a hat pulled low and a kerchief hiding all but the clear blue eyes.

Another man stalked out from behind the boulder, a slight breeze rustling his black jacket, a kerchief hiding his features too.

Hardy gulped. With a shaking hand, he wiped the cold sweat from his brow.

'You again,' he muttered.

Their pursuit slowing with every stride, Sheriff Creed and Deputy Fairborn rode a mile out from the mesa, then slowed to a halt. They both rubbed their brows as they stared at the deserted trail, the dispersing dust cloud ahead now the only remnant of their quarries' passage.

Thirty minutes earlier, Clayton Bell's gang of raiders had ambushed the wagon riders, the band that delivered cash to the banks along a 400-mile stretch of the Kansas Pacific railroad. In a short ambush that had cost them one man, they had stolen around $4,000.

But Creed reckoned that their type would probably view the cost as acceptable.

Ten miles on, three other groups of raiders had divided the pursuing forces with decoy runs. Although from the desperate way the men he was following galloped away, Creed was convinced that these men actually had the cash.

'You calling a stop?' Fairborn asked.

'For now.' Creed lowered the reins and hunched forward in the saddle. From the corner of his eye, he glanced back down the trail. 'We head back to Lincoln and round up a posse.'

'Agreed.' Fairborn sighed. 'We're just wasting our time here.'

As Creed nodded, the light wind carried a distant volley of gunfire from ahead. The blasts then echoed again and again as they faded to nothing through the surrounding craggy mountains. He snorted.

'Sounds like they're celebrating.' Creed sneered. 'Or taunting us.'

Another gunshot sounded, followed by two rapid shots.

'Or perhaps something else.' Fairborn narrowed his eyes and peered ahead, seeing no movement other than the swirling dust ahead. 'And I reckon we should find out what it is.'

With a shared nod, the two lawmen headed off the trail and hurried into the plains. After the short burst of gunfire, the only sounds were the rapid patter of their horses' hoofs.

A mile further on they approached a clump of trees beneath a rocky uprising. Numerous hoof-prints headed into the trees.

The lawmen slowed. They glanced at each other

and drew their guns, then one cautious pace at a time headed towards the trees.

Twenty yards from the trees, a splash of blood lay on the ground. Another splash was beside a huge boulder. Creed glanced to the left, then to the right and found more blood spotted in a trail that headed beyond the boulder.

With their guns held out before them, they edged their horses around the boulder, but aside from hoof-prints and blood, they found no horses or other signs of the raiders.

Then, fifty yards from the boulder, Fairborn saw a grizzled dead tree. From its branches something dangled, swaying in the breeze that whistled across the plains.

Edging his horse sideways, Fairborn rode to the tree, while Creed peered in all directions.

Closer to, he confirmed that the dangling object was a saddlebag. With a last glance around at the barren deserted plains, he holstered his gun and grabbed the bag. Then, with a swift gesture, he threw it open.

He whistled through his teeth, then swung the bag over his saddle and trotted back to join Creed.

'It's wads of dollars.' He tipped back his hat. 'The loot from the raid, I'm guessing.'

Creed glanced around. 'What are they doing? Why steal the cash, then leave it here for us to find?'

Fairborn furrowed his brow, then slipped the bag open and withdrew a handful of bills. He riffled through them, then thrust them back inside.

'I reckon I know what's happening here.' He

sighed and slapped his saddle. 'I reckon most of the cash is here, but some of it is missing.'

Creed leaned to the side and spat on the ground. 'The Ten Per Cent gang again,' he muttered.

CHAPTER 2

In Lincoln's bank, Sheriff Creed threw the saddlebag on to the clerk's desk and folded his arms.

The balding clerk, Jonah Eckstein, peered into the bag and withdrew a bundle of bills. He riffled through them, his stubby fingers whirring.

As he counted, Creed and Fairborn sauntered to the bank window and glared outside, sharing the occasional sigh until Jonah coughed and beckoned them to his desk.

Creed stayed by the window and folded his arms.

'How much did they steal?'

Jonah glanced down at his notes, then referred to a large ledger. He peered up over the top of his half-glasses.

'Four hundred and ten dollars – exactly ten per cent of the transported funds.' Jonah chuckled. 'If you haven't worked this out, I reckon I know who's responsible. The Ten Per Cent gang is always precise. They're never a percentage point out in either direction.'

Creed sneered. 'Nothing to admire there.'

Jonah widened his smile, but as Creed continued

to glare at him, he removed his glasses and polished them on his sleeve.

'I suppose you might not see events from a clerk's viewpoint. But I admire their precision.'

Creed strode across the office and peered down at the clerk.

'Perhaps if they like the number ten that much, we can hang them precisely ten times.'

Fairborn joined Creed and laughed. 'Or bring them in with precisely ten bullets in them.'

Jonah swung his glasses back on his nose and looked from one man to the other.

'You have no reason to do that.'

'We do,' Fairborn snapped. 'This is the third raid they've stopped in as many months.'

'But you won't act on the bank's behalf. We aren't pressing charges.'

'What?' Fairborn and Creed shouted together.

Jonah shuffled back on his chair and gulped.

'Transporting funds incurs plenty of expenses and ten per cent is a reasonable fee for recovering the cash from the clutches of Clayton Bell and his beastly raiders.'

'Those precise, fee-taking men are outlaws.' Creed swept the empty saddlebag to the floor. 'We'll bring them in.'

'But the bank has no problem with them. The matter is closed.'

Creed leaned on the desk, glaring into Jonah's eyes.

The clerk looked away and fiddled with his neck-tie, then looked back up to find that Creed was still glaring at him. He gulped and hung his head.

'The matter ain't closed.' Creed pushed back from the desk. 'I'll speak to your boss.'

Jonah glanced up. 'There's no need. He'll give you the same answer as I have.'

Creed slammed his fist against his thigh, then swirled round and strode to the door.

'You can't accept what they did,' Fairborn said. 'They still stole four hundred dollars from you and that's a crime even if you want to dismiss it as a delivery charge.'

Jonah waggled a stubby finger. 'They stole four hundred and ten dollars, and bounty hunters would charge a whole lot more to track down Bell's gang and with no assurance of recovering the stolen money.'

Fairborn snorted. 'We lawmen don't charge you anything.'

'Yes. But you never recover anything either.' Jonah smirked, then glanced away.

Fairborn glared down at the clerk's bald spot, then with an angry oath, turned and stormed for the door.

'Yet,' he muttered, joining Creed.

'Wait, Deputy.' Jonah uttered a short laugh, then masked it with a cough. 'Perhaps the bank might be interested in you finding the Ten Per Cent gang, after all.'

By the door, Fairborn turned. 'Glad you're seeing sense.'

'A big delivery passes through the county next month – perhaps fifty thousand dollars – and we'd like it to reach Denver safely. If we could hire the Ten

Per Cent gang to defend it, the bank might be prepared to pay ten per cent for their services.'

With his eyebrows raised, Fairborn glared back. Then a sly smile spread across Jonah's face.

Fairborn snorted and grabbed the door.

Outside, he took deep breaths and opened and closed his fists as he suppressed his anger. Creed joined him, his face as red as Fairborn's felt.

'Tell you one thing,' Fairborn muttered. 'The only person I hate more than Bell or the leader of the Ten Per Cent gang now is that smug clerk.'

'Yeah,' Creed muttered. 'Somehow, I'm going to wipe that irritating grin off his face.'

Twenty miles out of Lincoln, high in the hills, Nat McBain and Spenser O'Connor huddled around their small fire.

A night chill had descended quickly and a fierce wind was whipping the flames, but neither man wanted to risk attracting attention with a larger fire, preferring to huddle in his blanket instead.

Nat finished fingering a pile of bills and leaned back, smiling.

'How much?' Spenser asked.

Nat shuffled the bills into a neat pile. 'Four hundred and ten dollars – before expenses.'

Spenser snorted. 'Are you saying that you took ten dollars too much?'

'Nope. Four thousand one hundred dollars was in the saddle-bag.'

'You're precise.'

Nat shrugged. 'We have our name to live up to.'

'How much does that make in all?'

Nat rubbed his forehead. 'After expenses, fifty dollars shy of a thousand – not bad for three months' work.'

Spenser tapped his fingers, mouthing numbers. He wrapped his blanket around his shoulders more tightly and sneered.

'That means we've recovered nearly fifteen thousand dollars.'

Nat swung his blanket across his chest so that it tented around him.

'It does.'

'At this rate, we won't get enough money before our luck runs out.' Spenser slipped a hand from his blanket to rub his chin. He smiled, his teeth bright in the fire's glow. 'But I have an idea to speed things up.'

Nat blew out his cheeks and sighed. 'Go on.'

'We rename ourselves the Twenty Per Cent gang.' Spenser chuckled. 'Or even better we—'

'I can see where you're going with this.' Nat lifted a hand. 'But we ain't doing that. Ten per cent is the perfect amount to take. Any more and someone will take exception to the size of our cut, any less and it ain't worth our while.'

Spenser shook his head. 'It's an old argument but I still reckon leaving anything is a bad idea.'

Nat waved the pile of bills at Spenser. 'Taking *everything* is the bad idea. I got no desire to be a wanted man for the rest of my life.'

Spenser blew on his hands, then held them out to the fire.

'And I got no desire to end up dead. Every time we raid outlaws and return most of the cash, we take chances from every angle. Soon, our luck will run out.'

'It doesn't need to last for long. We just need two or maybe three more raids and we'll have enough cash to do anything we want.'

For long moments Spenser glared at Nat, then hugged his knees.

CHAPTER 3

A dozen whiskeys into the evening, Sheriff Creed slumped even further over the bar.

All around him, cowboys talked and laughed as they enjoyed their night out in the saloon. But Creed felt that every laugh was at his expense, that every argument concerned his failure to catch the vigilantes, and that every snatch of overheard conversation included the word 'ten'.

As Fairborn sauntered into the saloon and joined him at the bar, Creed poured himself another drink, then pushed his half-empty whiskey bottle to his deputy.

Fairborn poured himself a glassful and leaned on the bar. He fingered the glass as he considered Creed.

'You cheered up yet?'

Creed gulped his whiskey and blew out his cheeks.

'Nope. But I've drawn up a list of people I'm seeing on the day we slap the Ten Per Cent gang behind bars.'

Fairborn knocked back half of his whiskey.

'Been thinking about them. I reckon that clerk

might not be speaking for his bank. If we can speak to someone more senior than him, he might be annoyed enough to press charges.'

With an outstretched finger, Creed tipped back his hat and slumped even further over the bar.

'Might work, but I've been thinking along the same lines, and I reckon the man who is the most annoyed with them is Clayton Bell. If you can figure out what charges he might press, we might have a reason to go after them.' Creed laughed, the sound hollow.

Fairborn matched the grim humour with a low snort.

'Seems we'll just have to wait until there's another raid.'

'And we'll be behind Bell's raiders and even further behind the Ten Per Cent gang.' Creed glared around the bustling saloon. 'And everyone from that clerk to these nobodies will just reckon we're even bigger idiots.'

Fairborn gulped down his drink and poured another.

'Not everyone's mocking us like Jonah Eckstein did.'

'Perhaps not, but it just seems that . . .' Creed glared at a huddle of cowboys by the wall. He'd distinctly heard one of them say 'ten' then laugh.

'Forget it. You know how saloon talk starts. The Ten Per Cent gang is the latest novelty, but everybody's more excited by the mystery of who they are and what they'll do next. They aren't saying we're at fault.'

Creed snorted and pointed across the saloon. Fairborn followed his gaze.

Turner Galley was wandering to the bar with a lively grin on his face and a nearly empty bottle of whiskey dangling from his hand. Turner eyed Creed, then slipped the bottle on to the bar.

'You're looking mighty down this evening, Sheriff,' he said, tipping back his hat with a grimed finger.

Creed nodded. 'Got plenty of problems.'

'The Ten Per Cent gang?'

'Yup.'

'Then I got me a solution.' Turner wiped his mouth with the back of his hand, but it didn't remove the grin. 'This here Ten Per Cent gang is getting to all the outlaws before you do, right?'

Creed contemplated his glass, then leaned back on the bar.

'Yeah.'

'So why not deputize them? Then you'll have some of the finest lawmen around under your control, and you can take all the glory.'

Turner threw back his head and guffawed, slapping his stomach and stamping his feet as he exaggerated his mirth. Accompanying chortles rippled across the back of the saloon.

Creed sneered. 'You ain't funny.'

Turner slapped his knee. 'And you ain't no use as a lawman.'

In a large gulp Creed downed the remnants of his whiskey and pushed from the bar. He lifted a fist.

'Take that back.'

Turner's grin disappeared. 'Didn't mean anything by that, Sheriff. I was just jesting you.'

As Creed glared at Turner, Fairborn patted his shoulder.

'Ignore him,' he said. 'He's right. Turner's too stupid to mean anything by that.'

'Hey,' Turner whined.

'Then he shouldn't be jesting me.' Creed hitched his gunbelt higher. 'So I want an apology.'

Turner hung his head a moment, then looked up and nodded, the start of another grin twitching at the corners of his mouth.

'Perhaps I will.' Turner pointed at the bottle he'd placed on the bar. 'To show how sorry I am, I'll leave you the rest of my bottle of whiskey.'

Creed glanced at the bottle and nodded.

'That might just do it.'

Turner shook the bottle and held it up to light. He licked his lips and glanced over his shoulder, receiving a few chortles from his companions.

'Thought you'd appreciate that. It looks like there's ten per cent left in the bottle.' He chuckled, then grinned wider as Creed snorted.

Creed glanced at Fairborn, then with a backhanded lunge, slapped Turner's cheek.

The blow spun Turner, but on the second roll, he grabbed the bar and stopped himself falling. As his drinking partners shouted encouragement, he righted himself and rolled his shoulders, then charged Creed, flailing his fists.

Creed deflected the first two blows, then punched Turner deep in the guts. Turner rolled with the blow and staggered back a pace, but then stood his ground.

Two of his drinking buddies scraped back their chairs, but Fairborn strode from the bar and glared at them, his hand resting on his gunbelt and the calmest of smiles on his face.

With a few narrowed-eyed glances at each other, the men shuffled back behind their tables.

By the bar, Turner spat on his right fist and weighed in with a long round-armed blow, but Creed ducked under it and when he rose, he delivered a firm uppercut to Turner's chin with the flat of his hand.

Turner's head snapped back as he staggered a pace, flailing his arms as he fought to stay upright. He crashed into a table, scattering glasses, and leaned down a moment, regaining his breath.

He shook his head and turned, but Creed had advanced on him.

With the back of his hand, Creed delivered a slap to Turner's cheek that rocked him one way, and a firmer blow to his jaw with his left hand that knocked him the other way.

This time, Turner tumbled to the floor and lay rubbing his jaw.

Creed stood over him, his fists raised and his eyes bright.

'Come on,' he shouted. 'I'm just starting to get your jokes. Once I've knocked you down ten more times I might start laughing.'

Turner pushed to his knees. With his head lolling, he staggered to his feet only to receive another solid blow to the jaw that knocked him flat.

Creed loomed over him, but Turner's head lolled back. Creed spun round to place his back to the bar.

'Anybody else want to jest me,' he roared, 'because I'm in the mood for knocking a few smiles into oblivion.'

Most people turned their backs and hunched over their drinks or joined their colleagues in animated conversation. A few glared back, then shook their heads and returned to contemplating their drinks.

Creed kicked Turner in the side, receiving a groan.

'Then get up,' Creed muttered, 'so I can knock you down again.'

Fairborn sauntered to Creed's side.

'That's enough,' he whispered, laying a hand on Creed's shoulder. 'You've taught Turner the lesson he needed.'

Creed flinched from Fairborn's hand and strode over Turner's prone form to the bar. He grabbed Turner's whiskey bottle, knocked back half the contents, then thrust his legs wide and with his eyes blazing, glared at each person in the saloon in turn.

'I'm your lawman,' he roared, 'and nobody jests me.'

'That's enough, Sheriff,' the bartender said, ambling down the bar. 'This ain't you speaking. And I reckon in the morning you'll know that too.'

'That some kind of joke?' Creed roared. He swung round and glared at the bartender.

'Nobody here is looking for trouble but you.'

Creed gulped back the last of the whiskey from the

bottle, then threw it over his shoulder. As the bottle clattered to a halt in the corner of the saloon, he wiped his mouth and slammed a fist on the bar.

'Only thing I'm looking for is another drink.'

Fairborn shook his head and patted Creed's shoulder.

'Wes, I reckon you've had enough. A good—'

'I ain't had enough.' Creed waved his arms above his head. The gesture lurched him sideways so that he had to throw out a leg to avoid falling.

'Get him out,' the bartender muttered to Fairborn. 'He ain't drinking any more here tonight, or any other night until his mood's improved.'

As Creed glared at the bartender, Fairborn grabbed his elbow and dragged him back a pace, but Creed shrugged from Fairborn's grip and lurched back to the bar. He grabbed a whiskey bottle from the bar and with a last glare around the saloon, weaved a snaking route outside.

Fairborn mouthed an apology to the bartender, receiving a nod in return, and turned to follow Creed. But instead, he stopped in the doorway and watched Creed stagger down the road, throwing short punches at imaginary opponents.

With a long sigh, he strode back into the saloon and joined the two men who were checking on Turner.

CHAPTER 4

An hour into the cold morning, Sheriff Creed faced his first visitor of the day, Mayor Lynch.

Seated behind his desk in the sheriff's office, Creed nursed a strong coffee and a pounding headache. The mayor had already refused his offer of the former and his views on last night's incident in the saloon weren't helping the latter.

'Drunken fighting in the saloon,' Mayor Lynch shouted, slamming down his fist again and rattling Creed's desk. The sound reverberated deep into Creed's head. 'I can accept that happening in my town. But not when it's my lawmen who are starting it.'

'Don't suppose that anything I can say will help,' Creed said, pulling down his hat to shield his eyes from the harsh light.

With an angry lunge, Lynch knocked his hat off.

'One thing will help.'

Creed glanced at the hat on the floor, then folded his arms.

'I know. I'll bring in both Clayton Bell and the Ten Per Cent gang.'

'Nope. That won't impress me.' Lynch snorted and leaned on Creed's desk, shaking his head. 'But throwing your star on this desk *will* impress me. Then I can get a decent lawman in instead, who will catch Bell and won't start fights in saloons.'

'I ain't resigning. But I promise you I will bring in the outlaws.' Creed met Lynch's gaze a moment, then rubbed his raw eyes and lowered his head. 'And I won't start any more fights.'

'You're right. You won't start any more fights. Because if you do, I won't *wait* for you to resign.'

Creed looked up, his eyes blazing, his flash of apologizing forgotten.

'You can't run me out of office. I'm a democratically—'

'I can't, but I've had a dozen irate townsfolk complaining about you already today. One more brawl and I reckon they'll knock down your door and demand that you leave. And I'll be with them.' Mayor Lynch glared down at Creed, then stormed across the office. He stamped his feet as he halted in the doorway and glared at Fairborn. 'And don't think you'll be anyone's next choice for sheriff. Most people think you're as bad as Creed is.'

'They're wrong,' Fairborn snapped. 'I'm just as good as Creed is.' He looked Lynch up and down and sneered. 'And that's twice the man you'll ever be.'

Lynch snorted, then strode through the door, slamming it shut behind him.

'Thanks for the support,' Creed murmured.

Fairborn sauntered across the office to stand before Creed's desk.

'As your deputy, I'll support you, like I've always done. But as your friend, I'll tell you that Mayor Lynch was right. Sheriffs who start drunken brawls in saloons should throw in their stars.'

Creed glared back, then rolled from his chair and grabbed his hat. He swung it on his head and strode to the stove to pour himself another strong coffee. He hunched over it, then looked up and nodded.

'Aside from the mayor, you're the only man I wouldn't knock down for saying that.' Creed gulped a mouthful of coffee and slammed down the mug. 'But you're right. No more whiskey and no more taking it out on the wrong people.'

'Mighty glad to hear that.'

Creed punched his fist into his other hand.

'It's time we sorted out the real problem here.'

'Are you talking about Clayton Bell or the Ten Per Cent gang?'

'Bell ain't the real problem. He's just a lowlife. He'll get himself killed or caught before too long. But the Ten Per Cent gang is sorting out every crime around here before we get close to it. They're making us a laughing-stock.'

Fairborn sighed. 'And nobody but us cares that they take ten per cent.'

'Somebody else does care.' Creed licked his lips.

'Who you got in mind?'

Creed returned to his desk. He rummaged inside

and extracted a sheet of paper. He slipped it into his pocket and patted the pocket.

'My answer depends on how far you're prepared to go to improve your life.'

'You mean you're planning on doing something that could get your star turned in?'

By way of answer, Creed just raised his eyebrows.

With Fairborn at his side, Creed strolled into the bank. He threw the clerk's office door open and strode inside.

Jonah Eckstein looked up from his clear desk.

'I'm a busy man, Sheriff.' Jonah swiped away a layer of dust from his desk. 'You can come back later.'

'I ain't.' Creed dragged a chair from the wall. He slumped on it and glared at Jonah. 'I'm here for your help. We got far too many raids going on around here and they're escalating.'

'We've been over this.' Jonah tapped his fingertips together. 'The bank would prefer to receive everything we should, but faced with Bell's gang stealing everything, we'll gladly pay a small fee for the return of most of the funds.'

Creed scraped his chair closer to the desk.

'Perhaps, but outlaws get greedy.' Creed raised his eyebrows. 'And soon those small fees will become larger fees.'

'But as the bank aren't pressing charges, the Ten Per Cent gang aren't outlaws.'

Creed leaned back in his chair and crossed his legs. He glanced up at Fairborn, shaking his head.

'Anyone who flouts the law is an outlaw.'

'When drunken buffoons uphold the law,' Jonah said while he stared at his desk, 'most people would prefer the outlaws.'

'I'm no drunken buffoon.'

Fairborn sauntered to his side. 'He ain't. He just got down and he looked for someone to take it out on. And if you don't co-operate, I reckon you'll be next.'

Jonah glanced at Fairborn and sighed, then turned to Creed.

'Let's hear it, Sheriff. But make it quick. I'm a busy man.'

Creed took a deep breath. 'I want to set a trap for the Ten Per Cent gang.'

Jonah spread his hands wide. 'And?'

'And I need information on when the wagon riders' next shipment will be.'

Jonah snorted. 'I'm not giving you that.'

Creed rocked forward as if to rise. 'Then I'll ask your boss.'

'I've told you before. He won't be interested. But if you want to waste your time, do it.' With a slow shake of his head, Jonah pointed to the door. 'Just don't waste any more of my time telling me about it.'

Creed slapped both his knees and stood. He sauntered in a circle, then took two paces towards the door. He stopped.

'But I won't ask your boss about the next shipment. I'll discuss something far more interesting.'

From a drawer, Jonah bustled a handful of papers on to his desk, then looked up at Creed's turned back. He glanced at Fairborn, who shrugged.

'What will you ask him?'

Creed turned and raised his eyebrows. 'I'll ask him about your previous job.'

Jonah gulped. 'What's that supposed to mean?'

Creed extracted a sheet of paper from his pocket and walked over to Jonah's desk. He slammed it down, letting a fuzzy image of a face peer out between his outstretched fingers.

'It means that five years ago, you were a shipping agent in California, except your employment ceased when you was charged and sentenced for extortion, bribery, embezzlement and about another dozen crimes. If you haven't worked this out, I reckon that won't impress an employer of a clerk who has access to his money.'

Jonah stared at the poor impression of his own features, then sighed.

'If you tell him, he'll probably promote me. I only did what any shipping agent does to ensure the business operates effectively.'

'If you say so.' Creed slid the paper back into his pocket. 'I'll let him decide.'

With exaggerated slowness Creed straightened, then turned and paced to the door. He reached the door and stretched out a hand.

'Wait,' Jonah whispered.

Creed stamped his feet as he halted. He rocked back and forth, then slowly turned.

'Pardon?'

'I said, "wait".' Jonah edged his papers around his desk. 'A trap is a minor clerical issue. There's no need to involve anyone more senior than me.'

Creed smiled. 'I'm glad we have an understanding.'

CHAPTER 5

Ten miles out of Lincoln, Turner Galley's ramshackle smithy stood at the junction of the trails from Lincoln to Bear Creek and from Denver to Stone Creek. The early morning sun was glinting off Turner's display of assorted metalwork as Creed and Fairborn dismounted. They left their horses in a small corral at the side, then sauntered into the smithy.

From under a louring brow, Turner glared back and flexed his jaw.

'Last night ain't worth remembering as far as I'm concerned, Sheriff,' he said. 'Ain't no need to make things worse.'

'We ain't here to talk about last night.' Creed stood aside to let Fairborn follow him in. 'We're here to talk about trouble and how you're at the centre of most of it.'

'Typical. You're useless at tracking down outlaws so you harass me again.' Turner thrust a branding-iron into the brazier and sauntered two paces towards Creed, wiping his hands on his apron. 'Like I've told you a hundred times – I ain't a horse-thief.'

'You sell horses. And you don't always know where they come from.

'Made a few mistakes in the past, and you know about them. But I have a fine reputation now.'

Creed glared at Turner and snorted. With deliberate paces, he strode to a pile of metalwork, some rusty, some half-complete.

Creed picked up a lever. He opened and closed it, confirming it was a wagon brake, then threw it on the pile of metalwork and selected another.

'Aside from your *reputation*, you got some real skill with metal-craft.'

'I have and unless you're looking to buy something, I'd be obliged if you'd leave.' Turner pointed to the door. 'And leave the door open when you go and let the stink out of here.'

'I do have something in mind.' Creed licked his lips. 'I want to see Clayton Bell.'

'You've already seen me twice about him. But as you didn't listen before, I'll tell you again – I got no idea where he is and even if I did . . .' Turner looked Creed up and down and sneered.

'This time it's different. I ain't looking to arrest him. I just want to meet him.'

Turner smiled. 'After you hit me in the saloon last night, I reckoned you just didn't have a sense of humour. Seems I was wrong.'

'I'm serious. It's like this – you shoe horses, sell on a few. Metal is mighty hard to get hold of so you don't ask too many questions aside from . . . can my customers pay? And I guess in some cases . . . will they kill me if I don't help them? You know plenty about what goes on, but one word to me about what you know and you end up dead.'

Turner stared at the fire. 'I guess you've seen things right.'

'An arrest is the worst I can threaten you with, except as I have nothing on you, I'll have to release you.'

'You're speaking sense. A few nights in your cells or death ain't a difficult choice.'

'Except people around here don't like horse-thieves. When a man gets a reputation, he can find himself dangling on the end of a rope without the law getting involved.'

'Then I'm all right. I don't have that reputation.'

'But if I arrest you for horse-stealing, then let you go, arrest you tomorrow, then let you go, arrest you again, then . . . before long the rumours will start. Then the next time a horse goes missing, you'll get a midnight visit from some angry townsfolk with a rope in hand. Of course when they realize that you're innocent, they'll feel right sorry, but that won't worry you. You'll already have a stretched neck.'

Turner gulped. 'An interesting threat, Sheriff, but I still don't know where Bell is.'

'I only want to talk to him.'

Turner shrugged. 'What you got to talk about?'

Creed chuckled, a huge smile appearing.

'That question was your big mistake.' Creed nodded to Fairborn.

In three long strides, Fairborn stormed across the smithy. He grabbed Turner's arms and pulled them back behind his back, then swung Turner round to face Creed.

Turner struggled, then slumped on finding that Fairborn had a firm grip.

'What you mean?' Turner babbled.

'Before, I might have believed that you didn't know where Bell is. Now, I know that you know. And you'll tell me.'

'You can arrest me, but I'm telling you nothing.'

Creed nodded. 'That's only because you're more scared of what Bell will do to you than what I'll do to you.'

As Turner gave a short nod, Creed strode to the pile of branding-irons by the fire. He grabbed one, then dropped it, letting it clatter on the floor. He picked up a second and faced Turner, grinning.

Turner gulped. 'You wouldn't.'

Creed traced the brand's pattern. 'This is a good brand. A big T.'

With a long lunge, Creed thrust the brand deep into the fire.

'Don't think about doing that,' Turner whispered. He struggled against Fairborn's firm grip, but the deputy tightened his hold.

'I ain't started, yet.' Creed bent to the pile of brands and selected another one. 'Reckon as I might spell out your name on your hide.'

'You ain't scaring me, Sheriff.'

'I ain't aiming to scare you. I just want to talk to Bell.' Creed thrust the second brand into the fire and withdrew the first. He glanced at the reddening tip, then thrust it deeper into the fire. 'Only question is – how many letters do you get branded into your hide before you help me.'

'You're a lawman. You wouldn't.'

Creed glanced at Fairborn. 'You got a firm grip?'

'Yup,' Fairborn said with a pronounced gulp.

Creed strolled to Turner. With a firm gesture, he ripped open his shirt, exposing his chest and quivering guts. He sauntered back to the fire and extracted the brand, then spat on it. The glowing metal sizzled.

Creed turned and stared deep into Turner's eyes, grinning.

'Sheriff,' Turner whispered, his throat catching.

'You got something to say?' With deliberate slow paces, Creed strode to Turner, the brand at arm's length.

'Rot in hell, scum.'

'Anything else?' Creed swung his arm up towards the cowering black-smith.

Turner pushed back from the approaching brand, his whirling feet skidding on the floor, but he only flattened himself against the impassive deputy's chest.

'You wouldn't.'

Creed edged the brand forward, the heat blistering Turner's chest hairs. The hairs curled and spluttered away, a sharp burning odour rising.

'Another wrong guess.'

'All right,' Turner screamed. 'I'll do what you want.' Through wild eyes Turner watched Creed nod and withdraw the brand. He sighed. 'Just give me something to take to him.'

Creed glanced at the dulling end of the brand,

then walked back to the fire and thrust it back in.

'I want Bell to leave my county and pester someone else. I want to know what it'll take to do that.'

Turner snorted. 'I can answer that for nothing. He won't leave.'

'I ain't looking for *your* answer.' Creed grabbed the second brand and stoked it into the fire.

'I'll see him,' Turner shouted. 'But I ain't promising anything.'

Creed withdrew the heated brand from the fire and swung it round to aim it at Turner.

'Then I ain't interested.' He advanced a long pace towards Turner. 'I hope your second offer is better.'

'Stop! I'll be persuasive, honest I will, honest.' Turner glared at the brand until Creed lowered it. He gulped. 'Give me two days and I'll get back to you.'

'Don't want two days.' Creed advanced another pace and raised the brand. 'I want to see Bell, *now*.'

'That ain't . . .' Turner glared at the approaching brand. 'I'll do it.'

Creed grinned and to his nod, Fairborn released Turner, who stumbled to his knees.

On the floor, Turner wiped a layer of sweat from his brow. Then, with a last glance at the two lawmen, he scurried outside on hands and knees.

Creed moved to follow him, but Fairborn grabbed his arm and pulled him back.

'Got to ask you,' Fairborn said, 'would you have used the brand?'

Creed sauntered across the smithy and threw the cooling brand back on to the pile of branding-irons.

'You shouldn't be interested in my answer. When I started on this, I decided how far I was prepared to go.' Creed turned and strode to the door. 'Only thing you should worry about is how far you're prepared to go.'

CHAPTER 6

Twenty miles from Turner's smithy, deep into the hills, Fairborn and Creed sat astride their horses outside an abandoned farm.

'I've seen three rifles on us,' Fairborn whispered, leaning to Creed.

'If you've seen three,' Creed said, 'there must be at least twice as many you ain't seen.'

Fairborn glanced at the old man sitting on the main shack's porch. He was rocking back and forth with a blanket thrown over his legs, but he kept his hands beneath the blanket.

Outside the tumbledown barn, two men lounged, fingering their gunbelts, their narrow-eyed gaze never leaving the lawmen.

'I've trusted you enough to come here, but if you're wrong, I don't reckon I'll get enough time to regret trusting you.'

'Yeah, but if we live, this is one hideout Bell won't use again.'

'Glad you're thinking about the future.' Fairborn tipped back his hat. 'I'm just worrying about the next two minutes.'

With a sudden yell, a pale-faced Turner wheeled out of the shack propelled by a firm boot. He hit the ground, rolled, and came up with a resigned shrug. He coughed twice before he faced Creed.

'Bell will see you,' he said. 'But you leave your guns out here.'

Creed snorted and swung from his horse. He waited until Fairborn joined him.

'Stand tall and look confident,' he whispered from the corner of his mouth.

He brushed past Turner and on to the porch. He tipped his hat to the old man, then rolled his shoulders and kicked back the door. With his back straight, he strode inside.

Clayton Bell sat behind a table, the only furniture in the room. Trent Jackson, Clayton's ever-present hired gun, stood beside the table. Two other men flanked the doorway.

Creed paced into the room. Fairborn edged after him, keeping the men flanking the door in his view.

With his eyes narrowed, Bell looked Creed and Fairborn up and down. He smiled, the arc of yellow teeth breaking the mass of bristles and grime.

'Only seeing you because I didn't believe it really was you.' Bell gestured at Creed's waist. 'And you're packing a gun.'

Creed glanced at Trent. 'I'm no threat when your gunslinger is here.'

'You're right,' Trent muttered through gritted teeth. He drew himself to his full rangy height and blew on his fingers. 'Either of you makes a wrong move and you'll both be dead before you complete that move.'

Bell patted his grimed hands together. 'So why have you got yourself a death wish?'

'I ain't.' Creed slowly lifted his hands and folded his arms. 'I'm here to offer you a deal.'

'And when I don't like it?'

'If that happens, I'll leave.'

'You must be mighty confident I'll take it.' Bell glanced at Trent and chuckled, the sound harsh.

'I am confident.' Creed glanced over his shoulder. 'And it's a deal for your ears and Trent's ears only.'

'I hide nothing from my men.'

Behind Creed, the two men grunted their approval.

'You don't need them to guard us if you're as confident in Trent's abilities as you say you are.'

Bell glared back at Creed a moment, then nodded.

'Dave, Kyle, go,' he muttered.

With a shared grumble, the two men peeled from the wall and wandered outside.

Bell appraised Creed until the door slammed shut, then raised his eyebrows.

'When two men have a mutual enemy,' Creed said, 'they have something in common.'

'Which enemies do you have in mind?'

'The Ten Per Cent gang.'

For the briefest of moments, Bell's right eye twitched.

'I got plenty of reasons to hate them. But why do you hate them?'

'When men successfully take the law into their own hands, it suggests to everyone that vigilante justice is better than real justice. Before too long anarchy will descend, and I don't fancy picking up the pieces.'

Bell shrugged. 'Hard to care either way, but I believe you. So what are you offering?'

Creed took a deep breath. 'The Ten Per Cent gang is always ahead of you and they're even further ahead of me. So we lay a trap. You'll carry out a raid, except I'll know where and when, so when the Ten Per Cent gang raid you, I'll be waiting for them.'

A huge grin spread across Bell's face. He glanced up at Trent, who snorted a laugh. Bell turned back to Creed, shaking his head.

'You want me to tell you what I'm doing, just so you can lie in wait for . . .' Bell waved an arm at Creed. 'You must think I'm stupid.'

'I do, but I ain't interested in what you're doing.' Creed raised his eyebrows. 'I'm planning your next raid on the wagon riders.'

Bell lowered his elbows to the table and cradled his chin in his hand. With his other hand, he rubbed the bridge of his greasy nose using a steady rhythm, then looked up at Bell and shook his head.

'You're a straight lawman. You won't give me information on the wagon riders' movements.'

'I ain't. The shipment you'll raid won't have a dime in it.'

Bell laughed, Trent echoing his mirth.

'You expect me to risk my men to steal nothing,

then risk them further getting that nothing stolen off them?'

'You got it. You ain't as stupid as you look.' Creed glared down at Bell, who narrowed his eyes and gripped the side of the table. 'But the risk is minimal. The wagon riders will be in on the deal. Their gunfire will be token. The aim here is to capture the Ten Per Cent gang.'

With a steady rhythm, Bell tapped his fingers on the table. The fingers stopped moving and he looked up. He nodded.

'I've heard enough. And you got lucky. You've intrigued me enough to let you live. I'll discuss this with my men and get back to you.'

Creed snorted. 'You won't. This deal is between the four of us.'

'It ain't. Everyone has to agree.'

'Ridiculous.' Creed turned and took a long pace towards the door. 'Come on, Alan. I ain't wasting any more time with this idiot. All deals are off.'

Bell jumped up from behind the table and pointed a firm finger at Creed.

'Explain that or die.'

While shaking his head, Creed turned. He looked Bell up and down, sneering, then strode three paces and stood before the table.

'When Fairborn and me were together, Trent could kill us both before one of us killed you. But now we're ten feet apart, and Trent ain't taking both of us down before one of us wipes away your evil-smelling existence.'

Bell's eyes widened. 'You can try, but you'll live

longer if you explain.'

Creed glared back a moment, then shrugged.

'Why are the Ten Per Cent gang so successful?'

'They got lucky.'

'No.' Creed leaned forward and grinned. 'They got information.'

Bell winced. 'You saying that one of my men works for the Ten Per Cent gang?'

'Yup.'

Bell pouted, rocking his head from side to side.

'Perhaps you're right.' Bell rubbed a hand through his greasy hair, then shrugged. 'A two-man gang is too small to be *that* successful.'

'Only two men!' Creed shook his head as he blew out his cheeks and slammed his hands on his hips. 'Anybody seen either of them?'

'One's dark-haired, the other's blond, but they cover their faces and there's nothing familiar about them.' Bell glanced away a moment, then looked up at Creed, grinning. 'Except we've surmised one thing. If you want to know who runs the Ten Per Cent gang, look to your own kind.'

'Lawmen?' Fairborn snapped, speaking for the first time. 'You got proof?'

Bell turned his steady gaze from Creed.

'Nope, but if I raided a rival gang, I wouldn't leave anyone alive to come after me, but these men have raided us three times and they're yet to kill anyone – wounded a few, but no deaths. That speaks of principles.'

Fairborn lowered his head a moment, sighing.

'It could just mean more of your people are in

their pay than you thought.'

'No. These men tread a fine line. They keep just enough money to make it worth their while, but not so much that anyone reckons they're greedy. And they use just enough force to get the job done, but not enough that they risk the noose.'

As Fairborn nodded, Creed edged a pace closer to Bell.

'Do we have a deal?' he asked.

Bell patted his fingertips together, then nodded, but Trent sauntered round the table. He squared up to Creed and narrowed his eyes.

'If we work together,' he muttered, 'we ain't interested in seeing them behind bars.'

Creed smiled. 'Neither am I.'

CHAPTER 7

'I reckon you were right about Bell,' Fairborn said. 'He is stupid.'

'What changed your mind?' Creed asked.

Fairborn pointed down the side of the mesa to the trail below and the two riders galloping towards them.

'He always uses the same tactics. Man as predictable as that is just asking for someone to take advantage of him.'

In the week since Creed's and Fairborn's meeting with Bell, they'd avoided Mayor Lynch or the possibility of Creed getting into any more fights with the townsfolk by spending as much time as possible away from Lincoln.

Instead, they'd relayed messages through Turner to Bell, honing the last details of a raid in which most of the raiding party had to believe that the risks were high and the return was equally high.

Worse, Creed had dealt with Jonah Eckstein more often than was good for his fraying temper while the smug clerk confirmed details of the bogus cash shipment with Drago Holbeck, the leader of the wagon riders.

The previous night, the lawmen had slept on a flat length of rock high above the plains and from first light had watched the trail to Stone Creek, waiting for Bell to carry out the raid at the pre-arranged place.

On time, a wagon—a stagecoach with the top half sawn off – had trundled down the trail, a phalanx of dark-blue coated wagon riders on all sides. The bulky form of Drago Holbeck rode up front.

From either side of the wagon, two groups of raiders had peeled away from their hiding-place in a narrow gully and descended on the wagon. After a short chase, they had forced it to make a stand.

The wagon riders blasted off an impressive amount of high gunfire to satisfy anyone who was watching, either casually or not, of the raid's authenticity.

Although the wagon was too far away to see clearly, it didn't appear that the raid hurt anyone, but when Drago moved the wagon riders to a more defendable position, the wagon containing the cash became unhitched and rolled free.

A solid block of raiders swarmed over the wagon and with the wagon riders being slow to recover from their apparent mistake, Bell's gang grabbed the cash shipment within seconds. Then they rode away, throwing off the lame pursuit within a mile.

Half-way through the second mile, Bell's gang had split into four groups, each heading off in a different direction.

But the two men holding the fake cash swung in a long arc around the mesa, and hopefully straight into an ambush.

'Bell *is* predictable,' Creed said. 'So we get double the benefit from this. As soon as we have the Ten Per Cent gang, we'll have an advantage on Bell the next time he raids.'

Creed jumped to his feet and beckoned Fairborn to follow him.

The two lawmen slipped back from the edge of the slope, then dashed for their horses. They galloped across the mesa, down a steep gully, and across two ridges to reach a secure location. There, they could look down on the spot where Bell had ordered the men with the fake cash to wait.

For ten minutes the lawmen waited, then the two riders hurtled into sight, slowing as they reached the rendezvous point.

Fairborn nudged Creed. 'I've seen no sign of this ambush.'

'Guess that's why the Ten Per Cent gang is so successful. Nobody sees them until it's too late.'

The outlaws below halted and edged close to a large rock. They sat astride their horses, facing away from each other as they watched the trail in both directions.

There, they waited for the remaining parts of Bell's gang to meet them.

High above them, the lawmen waited for the Ten Per Cent gang to show.

In a bolt-hole in the canyon opposite the mesa, Nat

McBain and Spenser O'Connor peered out from their hidden position. They had been there, quiet and unmoving, since the lawmen had ridden on to the plains last night.

For the last hour, both men had communicated their views on Bell's raid using only sighs and slow shakes of the head.

Nat edged to the side and nudged Spenser.

'They really seemed to think that their fake raid would catch us,' he whispered.

'Yeah,' Spenser murmured. 'All that energy and planning for nothing.'

'Kind of makes me feel sorry for our lawmen.' Nat smiled and lifted a hand to his brow as he craned his neck. 'But not too much.'

An hour after the raid on the wagon riders, the decoy runners joined the other outlaws and they headed off.

The two lawmen glared at each other and nodded. In silence they mounted their horses and rode over the mesa, down to the trail on the opposite side, then headed at a fair trot back to Lincoln.

Eight miles out of Lincoln, two riders galloped towards them.

As the lawmen pulled their horses to a halt, Creed glanced around, but the approaching riders were the only people on the trail and the surrounding plains were clear.

'Reckoned as meeting Mayor Lynch was going to be mighty tough,' Creed said, 'but meeting Bell and Trent could be worse.'

Fairborn nodded to the tangle of rocks beside the trail.

'You reckon we should take cover?'

'Gunfire won't get us out of this. We need to talk tough.'

From ahead, Trent thrust up an arm and, a moment later, a gunshot whistled by two yards from Creed's head.

'Time for second thoughts,' Fairborn shouted. He yanked on the reins, his horse rearing as he turned it, wasting valuable seconds.

'Go for cover,' Creed shouted, leaping from his horse.

Fairborn calmed his steed as a second gunshot skimmed by his shoulder. He leapt from his horse, rolling as he hit the ground to slam into the tangle of boulders beside Creed. Wasting no time, he drew his gun and both men swung their guns on to the top of the rock.

Bearing down on them, Trent and Bell thrust out their guns at arm's length.

Creed and Fairborn narrowed their eyes, but they didn't fire as they waited for the outlaws to ride closer.

Ahead, the riders galloped at them, Trent blasting a round every few strides. Each shot whistled close by or plumed into the dust, but he was closing and so were the bullets.

Then Trent and Bell pulled back on the reins and halted just out of the lawmen's firing range.

'Sheriff,' Bell shouted, 'you made a big mistake.'

'We agreed on the plan,' Creed shouted. 'It ain't

our fault that it failed.'

'We did everything as agreed, and nobody showed.' Bell turned his horse to the side while Trent reloaded. 'No Ten Per Cent gang, nothing.'

Creed hung his head a moment, sighing.

'The plan should have worked. Information must have leaked out to the Ten Per Cent gang. Who did you talk to?'

Bell glanced at Trent and shrugged.

'Nobody but us knew. But as soon as my men find out that there's no cash, somebody will remember that I've been talking to you, and somebody will work out that the wagon riders gave up the cash too easily. And I'll have plenty of trouble.'

'Next time, we just have to—'

'There ain't no next time.'

A round of gunfire peppered the rock and in self-preservation, Creed and Fairborn hurled themselves to the ground. As soon as one volley ended another volley started.

They cringed as they waited for an opening, and when it came, they swung up in unison and fired in an instant, but Trent and Bell were already galloping away.

As Fairborn lowered his gun, Creed blasted twice at their receding backs. Then they both slumped to their knees together.

'Suppose we were lucky,' Fairborn murmured. 'Trent is a good enough shot to take us when we gave an opening.'

Creed glanced over his shoulder and snorted.

'We weren't lucky. Trent always hits what he aims

at, and he wasn't aiming at us.'

Fairborn narrowed his eyes, then swirled round. He winced.

At least a quarter of a mile away, their untethered horses were now hurtling across the plains away from them, nothing in their headlong dash suggesting they'd be easy to catch.

'Guess we'd better start on that walk.'

Creed sighed. 'At least it'll postpone meeting Mayor Lynch a while longer.'

Fairborn rolled to his feet. 'And perhaps if we're real lucky, he won't get to hear about what's just happened.'

Creed snorted and jumped to his feet. 'I just don't reckon our luck is that good at the moment.'

CHAPTER 8

Sheriff Creed and Deputy Fairborn staggered into Lincoln, footsore and weary, irritation and brooding anger bowing their shoulders. They headed straight for the sheriff's office, but Mayor Lynch ran from his offices and waylaid them in the road.

'You'd better round up a posse quickly,' he shouted, gesturing up and down the road. 'Clayton Bell raided the wagon riders.'

Fairborn leaned to Creed and sighed. 'Seems you were right. We ain't getting any luck these days.'

'Luck,' Lynch shouted. 'This has nothing to do with luck. You need to sort this out.'

Creed lifted his right leg and laid a scuffed boot over his left knee.

'Done all the sorting out I aim to do for one day.' He prised his foot from his boot and batted a pile of dust on to the road.

'Stop wasting time!' Lynch set his hands on his hips. 'Clayton Bell is getting away. I've had enough of waiting for the Ten Per Cent gang to bail you out. Get your boots on and this time—'

'This time, the Ten Per Cent gang didn't show.'

Creed swung into his boot and emptied the second boot.

'Then do something. Bell's gang will—'

'I'm doing nothing. I'd set a trap, except the Ten Per Cent gang didn't spring it.'

Lynch slapped his palm against his forehead.

'You mean you knew all about the raid?'

'Yeah. I agreed with the bank that there'd be no cash to steal.' Creed slipped into his second boot. 'But the Ten Per Cent gang figured it out and didn't raid Bell's gang.'

'And this was all your idea?' Lynch shouted.

Creed tipped back his hat. 'Yeah.'

Lynch threw his hands above his head. 'And the ridiculous thing is, you're proud of it.'

Creed rubbed his chin, then nodded. 'I am. And if it'd worked, you'd like the sound of it too.'

'You're wrong, and as it didn't work, everyone will reckon you're an even bigger fool than before.'

'They won't,' Creed snapped. He glanced along the deserted road. 'Only the bank, Deputy Fairborn, and you know that it was a trap.'

'Everybody's knows about the raid on the wagon riders.' Mayor Lynch turned on his heel. 'The truth won't stay hidden.'

With all but Trent and Bell gathered at the meeting place high in the hills, Hardy Newman ripped open the captured saddlebag. His discovery of the cut newspaper within initiated a round of glaring, recriminations and arguments that festered for the next hour.

Eventually, Deke Pewter passed a bottle of whiskey around.

Even with this, everyone drank in sullen silence.

'I can't believe we stole nothing,' Kyle Samuels muttered. He sat, perched the saddlebag between his legs, and ripped out yet another handful of newspaper.

Hardy slumped down beside him and forced a wan smile.

'Cheer up. At least the Ten Per Cent gang didn't raid us.'

Kyle hurled the paper over his head. It showered around him as he turned to Hardy, his eyes blazing.

'That supposed to be funny?'

Hardy blew out his cheeks and hung his head.

'Perhaps.'

Kyle stabbed a finger against Hardy's chest.

'Do I look amused?'

Hardy glanced up, shaking his head. 'You're mighty annoyed. Just like me and everybody else here.'

As grumbles rippled around the men, Kyle grabbed another handful of paper from the saddlebag and thrust it into Hardy's face.

'But I don't reckon you're as annoyed as I am.' Kyle glanced around, receiving sullen stares. 'Or anyone else here.'

'Be quiet,' Carlos Pitcairn shouted, passing the whiskey bottle on to Slim Johnson. 'You're just looking for a fight and nobody's interested.'

'I ain't looking for a fight. I just want Hardy to answer my question.' Kyle rolled to his feet. He set his feet wide and slammed his hands on his hips. 'So are you as annoyed as everyone else here?'

'What's that supposed to mean?' Hardy asked, glaring at Kyle.

With a short lunge, Kyle grabbed Hardy's collar. He ruffled it shut and pulled him forward so that he could glare deep into his eyes.

'It means I want to know where the cash is.'

'I know as much as you do.' Hardy batted Kyle's hand away.

Kyle sauntered around Hardy, waving his handful of paper.

'Except you hid for an hour. You had enough time to hide the cash.'

'That's rot.'

Hardy glanced around, but this time the glares he received were not so apathetic. Several men were muttering to each other. Others rolled to their feet and shuffled towards him.

Carlos took a long pace forward to stand beside Kyle.

'Kyle's right,' he said. 'You had enough time to hide the cash. And we only have your word that the Ten Per Cent gang raided you the last time.'

Hardy clutched his bandaged shoulder. 'Except they shot me and Fletcher to hell. You and Carlos lost the loot the first time and I don't see any bullet wounds on you. What happened? Were you too scared to shoot each other to make it look like they raided you.'

Carlos's eyes blazed. 'That's dangerous talk.'

Hardy edged his hand down to his gunbelt.

'It is. But I reckon I'll put a few bullets in you to even things up.'

'You can try,' Carlos muttered, swirling round to face Hardy.

'Wait!' Fletcher shouted. 'Bell and Trent are returning.'

Hardy glanced away from Carlos to see two men riding towards them. He turned back to glare at Carlos.

'This ain't over. I reckon you got some questions to answer.'

Bell and Trent rode into the campsite and pulled their horses to a halt.

'What's happening?' Bell shouted.

'We're just trying to work that out,' Hardy muttered. 'But if you give me some room, I'll get some answers soon enough.'

Bell jumped from his horse. 'What's he mean, Kyle?'

Kyle waved his handful of paper, then slammed them to the ground.

'The cash shipment was just newspaper. Somebody duped us. It could have been the wagon riders, but Carlos has the idea that it was Hardy, and Hardy has the idea that it was Carlos.'

Bell looked at each man in turn. 'Ain't no need for you to shoot each over this. It was my mistake. I did a deal with the wagon riders for them to surrender the shipment, except I now reckon that they fooled me. The real shipment is probably getting through somewhere else.'

'They duped us.'

'They didn't.' Bell tipped back his hat. 'They duped me. And I'll sort this out. It won't happen again.'

'It won't,' Hardy snapped.

Bell turned to Hardy. 'What's that mean?'

Hardy hitched his jacket closed and stood straight.

'I reckon a man who gets duped can't give other men orders.'

With his eyes blazing, Bell paced towards Hardy and stood before him, glaring deep into his eyes. Trent joined him to stand two paces to his right.

Hardy stood his ground and folded his arms.

Bell glanced away then, with the back of his hand, slapped Hardy's cheek.

Hardy staggered to the side, Trent grabbing him. With a lightning gesture, Trent ripped his gun from its holster and slammed the barrel into Hardy's temple.

'And I reckon you got some apologizing to do,' he whispered into Hardy's ear.

Trent spun Hardy round so that his back was to him, then glared around the remainder of the group. His lips curled with the harshest of smiles.

Hardy glanced around, searching everyone's eyes as he judged his chances. He took a deep breath.

'That ain't happening. There's fifteen of us and two of you.'

'Perhaps. But you'll die first.'

'I will, but you'll follow me in seconds.'

'Stop!' Bell shouted, raising his hands. 'Nobody is killing anybody. If we work together, we can get what we want.'

Everyone glanced at everyone else. Most men gave small nods and backed, but Carlos leapt forward.

'No,' he shouted. 'We ain't getting what we want working for you. Between the Ten Per Cent gang and those double-crossing wagon riders, we ain't had a success in months. I'm with Hardy. We need a new leader.'

'And you're putting yourself forward, are you?'

Carlos squared off to Bell. 'Yup. When Trent kills Hardy, one of us will kill Trent. Then you and I will decide which one of us leads what's left.'

Bell rubbed his chin as he glared around the men facing them. He shrugged, then charged Carlos with his hands raised clawlike and aiming for Carlos's throat.

In a sudden lunge, Carlos thrust up both his arms and knocked Bell's hands away.

As Trent tightened his grip around Hardy's shoulders, Bell hurled a huge punch at Carlos's head.

Carlos ducked the punch, but Bell barged into him and with his right shoulder, bundled him to the ground, then hurled himself on top of Carlos's supine form.

Each man grabbed the other man's neck and tried to wrestle himself on top, throwing up huge gouts of dust as they rolled back and forth.

Then Carlos struggled out from under Bell, leapt on his back, and slammed his head down into the dirt.

In Trent's grip, Hardy squirmed, taking Carlos's sudden supremacy as his chance to grab his freedom, but with a twist of his hand Trent blasted

Hardy in the head. With a contemptuous lunge, Trent pushed Hardy's lifeless body away and roved his gun back and forth across the arc of men facing him.

As one, everyone hurled their hands to their holsters, but Trent blasted a bullet through Stone Meadow's guts and with a series of flinches, everyone raised their hands.

Trent smiled, then aimed his gun at Carlos's and Bell's fight.

Now Bell had prised Carlos's grip away from his head and was slowly pushing him to the side.

Trent centred the gun on Carlos's head, waiting for an opening.

Then in a sudden lunge, Bell hurled Carlos away.

Carlos landed on his back, but Bell leapt to his feet, blocking Trent's view of Carlos, and reached down to grab Carlos's collar. He pulled him to his feet and held him upright, then with a long slug to the jaw, knocked Carlos on his back.

Even as Carlos slid to a halt, Trent blasted lead into his forehead.

As Carlos twitched, then lay still, Trent and Bell backed to stand together.

'Anyone else fancy questioning who should give the orders around here?' Trent roared.

Everyone glanced at the others, then disbanded, shaking their heads.

Kyle kicked the saddlebag away, scattering paper in a long arc.

Bell nodded. 'Hardy and Carlos were troublemakers. You men ain't like them. And with them gone, there'll be more money for the rest of us.'

'Or more of nothing,' Fletcher whispered, then hung his head.

CHAPTER 9

Mayor Lynch had promised that Creed's failed trap would become common knowledge quickly.

He was right.

Whether the information leaked from him or Jonah Eckstein, neither Creed nor Fairborn could tell. They suspected that it was both of them, but this suspicion didn't comfort them as they ran the daily gauntlet of sneers and snide remarks.

'Sheriff, you set any good traps recently? I hear you couldn't catch a dead prairie dog.'

'Hey, Ten Per Cent Sheriff, hope they ain't paying you more than ten per cent of a lawman's wage.'

'Fairborn, you like working for an idiot?'

The townsfolk hurled these comments and a whole lot worse at both lawmen daily.

Starved of sufficient pride to offer retorts, both lawmen spent less time patrolling Lincoln and the surrounding trails and spent more time brooding in the sheriff's office, hoping the abuse would end.

If it were, it was taking its time.

Two weeks after the failed trap, Creed slammed his feet down from the desk, tipped back his hat, and sauntered to the door.

'I'm tired of hiding in here. It's time we left.'

Fairborn looked up from under his hat. 'Abuse ain't over yet. This morning, Turner Galley told me that he was thinking of robbing a bank because the lawmen in Lincoln were so stupid he'd get away with it.'

'You should have arrested him for inciting trouble.'

'After your fight with him in the saloon, I didn't think we dare annoy the townsfolk any more.'

'True, but we can't avoid our duty, so we grit our teeth and go about our jobs.' Creed smiled and widened his eyes.

'I know that expression.' Fairborn rolled from his chair and stood. 'I reckon you've had an idea as to how we can change our fortunes.'

Creed rubbed his chin, nodding, then patted Fairborn's arm.

'Before I got us involved with Bell, I told you to decide how far you were prepared to go. I reckon you need to do that again.'

Fairborn sighed. 'I like being a lawman, but unless people start having faith in us, I won't be one for much longer.'

'Then come with me. It's time we set a bigger trap.' Creed opened the door and strode into the doorway. He glanced up and down the road. 'And this time, we'll net everyone.'

'You ain't thought this through,' Jonah Eckstein said. He edged a sheet of paper on his desk an inch to the side. 'And as I've plenty to do, I'd be obliged if you didn't waste any more of my time.'

'I have thought this through,' Creed muttered. He slammed both hands on Jonah's desk and leaned over it, forcing the balding man to cringe from his glaring eyes. 'The trap we set for the Ten Per Cent gang failed. Everybody reckons it was my fault, but I reckon information leaked out. And I don't have to look far for the culprit.'

Jonah removed his glasses and polished them furiously on his sleeve.

'You'd better not be looking at me.'

Creed grabbed Jonah's arm, stopping his polishing.

'I ain't looking any further than you. I reckon a toad like you would profit from what I tried to do.'

'You got proof?'

'Nope, but I reckon I can shake it out of you.'

With a snap of his wrist, Creed removed his hand from Jonah's arm and cracked his knuckles.

Jonah stared at the hand a moment, then gulped and hooked his glasses around his ears.

'You're right. Information about the bogus cash shipment did leak out. It just surprises me that it took you so long to figure out what was always obvious to me.'

Creed pushed up from the desk. With his eyebrows raised, he glanced at Fairborn.

His deputy shook his head and tutted.

Creed walked in a circle, slamming his fist against his thigh. When he'd completed a full circle, he set his hands on his hips.

'Go on, toad. Spell it out.'

Jonah leaned back in his chair, a smug grin plastered across his chubby face.

'The wagon riders deliver money at different times using different methods on different routes, yet every so often they get raided. How does that happen?'

Creed shrugged. 'I guess lookouts see them coming.'

'Perhaps,' Jonah said adopting a lecturing tone. 'But Bell only raids the largest shipments and that implies he has inside information on their size.'

Fairborn pushed from the wall and sauntered to Creed's side.

'And you know about their size beforehand,' he mused.

Jonah looked from one man to the other. He shook his head.

'I can see you want me to be the cause of your troubles, but I reckon I've understood what's happening here. The Ten Per Cent gang get information from Bell's gang, and Bell's gang get information from the wagon riders.'

'You smug varmint,' Creed snapped. With a long swipe, he hurled the papers from Jonah's desk. As they fluttered to the floor, he slammed down his fist. 'Information may leak out from many places, but it also leaks from you. What did you tell the Ten Per Cent gang?'

Jonah gulped and dropped to his knees. He grabbed the nearest sheet of paper, but Creed stormed around the desk and dragged him from the floor by his collar. He lifted him until the small man stood on tiptoes.

'Someone came to see me,' Jonah whined, his shoulders slumping in the sheriff's grip. 'He wanted to know about the last shipment.'

Creed hoisted Jonah a fraction higher, then snorted and threw him to the floor.

'Your information caused me a whole mess of problems.'

'It didn't.' Jonah rolled to his knees, sweat beading his brow. I just confirmed what he already knew. I'd never do anything that could get people hurt. I got ethics.'

'You got ethics! I'll give you . . .' Creed lifted his fist, but as Jonah hurled his arms above his head, he lowered it. 'You ain't worth it.'

Creed turned away, sneering, letting Fairborn walk past him.

'What did this person look like?' Fairborn asked.

Jonah lowered his arms and bustled across the floor, collecting the strewn paper.

'I didn't see him. He stayed in the shadows.'

'I don't believe that,' Fairborn snapped.

'I do,' Creed said with a snort. 'This toad ain't interested in what someone looks like. He only looks at their money.'

'You're right,' Jonah whispered. He rescued the last of his paper and deposited the bundle on his desk.

With deliberate paces, Creed swaggered across the office. He rounded the desk, forcing Jonah to back until he slammed into the wall. With a swift gesture, he lifted his hand, Jonah cringing, but he just tipped back his hat.

'Tell me, toad, since the last raid, has your contact seen you again?'

Jonah's gaze darted around the office, finding Fairborn, who planted his legs wide and folded his arms. Jonah hung his head.

'Yeah,' he whispered.

Creed lifted on his heels so that he stared straight down on the top of Jonah's balding pate.

'And did he ask about the next shipment?'

Jonah wiped a layer of sweat from his brow.

'Yeah, but like I said, I got ethics. I wouldn't do anything that could cause harm. He already knew it'd be a big one, and that it'd be by train on the twentieth. He was just confirming facts and—'

'Quit your excuses.' With the back of his hand, Creed slapped Jonah's shoulder, the minor blow still sending Jonah reeling. 'You're a toad. And that's official.'

Creed turned and sauntered across the office. With a snorted chuckle, he batted the papers from Jonah's desk again and with Fairborn strode outside.

On the boardwalk, both men leaned on the bank wall.

'Can you trust anything that toad's just told us?' Fairborn asked, breaking the irritated silence.

'Aside from you, I'm trusting nobody at the moment.' Creed pushed from the wall and turned to Fairborn. 'And I want to continue relying on your impartial advice, so I want you to do what a lawman does – investigate. We reckon that the members of

Ten Per Cent gang are ex-lawmen. Check that out and see where it leads you.'

'If I don't have to deal with the likes of Jonah Eckstein, that's the best plan you've had so far.' Fairborn smiled. 'What're you doing?'

'I'm dealing with the toads.' Creed tipped his hat and set off down the road.

CHAPTER 10

On the third of the month, Creed visited Turner Galley's smithy.

Turner was hammering a sheet of metal flat across his bench.

'What you want?' Turner muttered, looking up from his bench. He threw down the hammer.

'I'm visiting my old friend.'

While keeping his gaze on Creed, Turner edged to his brazier. He extracted a glowing poker and held it before him.

'Your last visit nearly cost me my life.' Turner snorted and poked at the fire. 'And it still might. So whatever you want me to do, I ain't interested. Go. And this time, don't return.'

Creed glanced at the door, then strode a long pace into the room.

Turner slipped out his poker again. The end glowed deep red as he held it at arm's length.

Creed glanced at the poker and smiled.

'But this time, I'll have to return to take delivery of the something you'll build for me.'

Turner glanced away a moment. With a shake of

his head, he thrust the poker into the fire and folded his arms.

'You ain't listening to me. I ain't doing any favours for you.'

'No favours, just business.' Creed raised his eyebrows. 'And for business, I'll pay half now, half on completion.'

Turner's gaze darted from the sheriff to his fire as he rubbed his chin. Then he shrugged and wandered back to his bench.

'What you got in mind?'

Creed extracted a slip of paper from his pocket. He sauntered to the bench and spread it out.

Turner edged around the bench to join Creed and peer at the paper. With a dirty finger, he traced over Creed's diagram.

'For this, one hundred dollars and two months to make it.'

Creed dragged the paper from under Turner's grip.

'Twenty-five dollars and you have sixteen days.'

Turner grabbed back the paper. 'Seventy-five and I'll meet your deadline.'

'Twenty-five, plus another twenty-five to buy your discretion. This deal is private between you and me.'

Turner rubbed a shaking hand through his hair.

'If you're talking about me seeing Bell again, that ain't happening. I don't ever want to see him again.'

Creed chuckled. 'In that case, I don't need to pay the extra twenty-five.'

Turner winced. 'People always say I talk too much.'

*

Creed sauntered into his office, whistling.

Fairborn looked up from his desk. He grinned and waggled a sheet of paper when he saw that Creed was smiling with more than just his mouth for the first time in months.

'What you found?' Creed asked.

'Nothing confirmed.' Fairborn placed the paper on his desk and turned it round. 'But I have a theory.'

Creed leaned down to read Fairborn's notes.

'Deputy Nathaniel McBain. You reckon he's our man?'

'Could be. He's fair-haired, like one of the Ten Per Cent gang.'

'You'll need more than that to convince me.'

'I have more. He worked for Sheriff Cassidy Yates.' Fairborn glanced at his notes. 'He now works in Monotony.'

'Yates, Yates?' Creed said, rubbing his chin. 'Did he work with Marshal Devine?'

'Yup.'

Creed whistled through his teeth. 'Now there's a tough lawman. If our man is McBain and some of Devine rubbed off on him, he'll take some beating. Why do you think it's him?'

'His father, Brett McBain, was an outlaw. He died during a raid on the wagon riders. Perhaps Nathaniel has a score to settle.'

'Like the sound of this. Go on.'

'Nathaniel was a deputy lawman for a year, but he handed in his badge. His excuse was the poor pay.' Fairborn looked up and licked his lips.

'That ain't a valid reason.'

Both men shared a laugh as Creed sat on the edge of the desk.

'McBain joined a bounty hunter, Clifford Trantor, to track down Kirk Morton, the leader of an outlaw gang that specialized in train raids. They all more or less wiped each other out along with the sheriff of Harmony. As everybody was double-crossing each other, nobody followed up the lawman's death too much.'

'So far, so believable.'

Fairborn leaned back in his chair. 'Nathaniel left Harmony with someone who resembled one of Kirk's men, Spenser O'Connor, even though they'd supposedly hung Spenser in Beaver Ridge jail a week earlier, but I reckon someone did something sneaky and he is Spenser.' Fairborn leaned back in his chair and raised his eyebrows. 'And he ain't the only member of Kirk Morton's gang that escaped. Two of his men are now working for Bell.'

'Why does that make you think Spenser is our man?'

'Because information is sneaking out from Bell's gang and it might be passing between old friends.' Fairborn held out a slip of paper.

Creed took the paper and read the two names on it.

'This sounds plausible. We have a lawman who's more interested in the pay than the law. He teams up with an outlaw who has no qualms about using his own kind.' Creed shuffled further on to the desk. 'And the best thing about it is, they're the kind of men we can defeat.'

'What's your plan?'

'I ain't got all the details.' Creed shuffled from the desk and strolled to the window. With his arms folded, he stared outside where dusk was shrouding Lincoln. 'But I can picture what two such men are thinking right now. In each raid they've acted with principles and not killed – that'd be our ex-lawman Nathaniel's idea. The double-crossing within Bell's gang and buying information from toads like Jonah Eckstein will be Spenser's contribution.'

Fairborn stood and joined Creed at the window.

'How does knowing that help?'

Creed unfolded his arms, his shoulders relaxed. He patted Fairborn's arm.

'Imagine you're Nathaniel. You're a decent lawman, but your colleague is as sneaky as they come.'

'That'd take some imagining,' Fairborn mused. He glanced at Creed and smiled.

'You can still try.' Creed winked.

Fairborn stared through the window, nodding to himself.

'I reckon they argue a lot. Their plan to keep just ten per cent is Nathaniel's idea, but Spenser ain't happy with it.'

'Now you're thinking.'

Fairborn pressed his cheek to the window to peer down the road where the distant mountains were outlined against the darkening sky.

'And as we speak, they're sitting around a campfire discussing how they'll best Bell next time, except

Spenser is getting unhappier and unhappier. He hates the ten per cent return rule. He says they should keep it all and take their chances.'

'But each time, Nathaniel talks him down.'

'And each time, Spenser gets a little closer to taking Nathaniel on. But Nathaniel's stronger than Spenser, so Spenser's waiting for the right moment.' Fairborn leaned back against the window frame and smiled. 'So we just need to know what it'll take to make Spenser face up to Nathaniel.'

Creed turned from the window and patted Fairborn's back.

'And we both know what that is and when it's coming.'

In the hills above Lincoln, Nat McBain and Spenser O'Connor sat around their spluttering camp-fire.

Both men sat on opposite sides of the fire, glaring at each other through the flames, the weak fire warming them less than their long-festering argument.

'That plan won't work,' Nat muttered, slamming his fist into his other palm.

'It will,' Spenser snapped, jumping to his feet.

'Quit arguing. We stick to what's worked in the past.'

'I got no desire to end up dead.' Spenser slammed his hands on his hips. 'And I reckon it's the same for you.'

Nat glared up at Spenser until the other man sat.

'And your plan will get us there even faster than anything else we might do.' Nat rolled on to his haunches and stoked the fire. 'This discussion is closed. We ain't doing that.'

Spenser glared at Nat, then with an angry lunge, spat into the fire and rolled on to his back to stare at the stars.

CHAPTER 11

At sundown on the nineteenth of the month, Creed rode a borrowed cart into Lincoln after his short trip to Turner's smithy. This afternoon, Turner had completed Creed's work and exactly as Creed had specified.

Creed jumped from the cart and sauntered into the bank.

Two minutes later, he emerged. In a large hand, he clutched Jonah Eckstein's collar and dragged him, with his legs whirling, into the road. Beside the cart, Creed released his grip and pointed at the five foot by four foot by three foot metal strongbox on the back.

'Impressed?' Creed vaulted on to the cart and patted the side of the box, a satisfyingly solid noise returning. 'I reckon that Turner did a good job here for once in his worthless existence.'

'I reckon he did.' Jonah shrugged his collar straight and leaned over the side of the cart to pat the box too. 'How much did you pay for it?'

Creed grinned. 'Twenty-five dollars.'

A huge smile emerged, which Jonah wiped away with a rub of his hand.

'Turner scammed you there.'

Creed glared down at Jonah. 'I did some mighty fine negotiating. I had to knock him down from one hundred.'

Jonah licked his lips. 'I'd have got it for less, perhaps for free.'

'How?'

'Under the promise that he'd be the first person the other banks would hire when they requested similar boxes. I'd hint the total order might be for anything up to fifty boxes.'

'But there are no further orders . . .' Creed contemplated Jonah's smug grin. 'I *was* right to see you. You're just the sort of sneaky toad I need.' Creed jumped down from the cart. 'And I hope you like your new strongbox. Turner built it to last. It'll make a fine addition to your bank. Sorry I couldn't get it any cheaper than twenty-five dollars.'

'I got a safe and it's better than . . .' Jonah hung his head as Creed widened his eyes. 'It's a fine box. I'll get your twenty-five dollars.'

Jonah turned to enter the bank, but Creed grabbed his arm and swung him back.

'I don't need the money yet. You can pay when we return.'

'Return from where?'

'Ensuring that one cash delivery gets through the county safely.'

Jonah snorted and glanced at the strongbox.

'And you reckon that box will help?'

Creed removed his hand and wiped it on his jacket.

'That and some help from a sneaky toad like you.'

With the strongbox on the cart behind him, the grinning sheriff and the glum Jonah travelled through the night to Restitution, one hundred miles beyond the Marren County border.

They headed for the train station and grabbed a few hours' sleep while they waited for the train to Denver.

An hour after dawn, the whistle from the approaching train awoke them as it arrived, on time.

The train had three passenger carriages, each half-full, and two transportation carriages with long doors on either side.

Horses bustled in the carriage nearest the engine.

The wagon riders had commandeered the second carriage, their dark-blue jackets appearing even darker in the sallow early-morning light.

They either jumped down on to the platform to flank the long front door, or sat with their legs dangling outside. Each man watched the movements of the scattered people on the platform, their rifles rested across their laps or swung up on a shoulder.

Creed ordered a porter to load the strongbox on to the first passenger carriage. Jonah followed on behind, but Creed slammed a hand on his shoulder and turned him towards the wagon riders' carriage.

'Time to you prove your worth,' Creed said. He patted Jonah's shoulder and urged him forward.

With a deep sigh, Jonah sauntered up to the lead

wagon rider, Drago Holbeck, and smiled.

'What do you want?' Drago muttered, drawing himself up to his considerable height.

'That depends on how amenable you are,' Jonah murmured, backing a pace when Drago loomed over him. 'We humbly request that—'

Creed brushed Jonah aside and snorted.

'He means,' he said, 'that we're helping you guard this shipment.'

Drago glanced at Creed's star and sneered.

'We don't need help from a lawman.' He narrowed his eyes. 'And you ain't even Sheriff Wilson.' Drago looked over Creed's shoulder at the station clock. 'But I have enough time before the train leaves to see what he has to say about you trying to act in his territory.'

'There's no need. I'm only here to help you.'

Drago spat a large gob of spit on the platform, inches from Creed's boots. He looked him up and down and chuckled without humour.

'I don't need your *help*.'

Creed rolled his shoulders to stand as tall as possible. Still, he was a half a head smaller than Drago was.

'And I reckon you do. You've already had more than one shipment raided in my county, and I don't want another *mishap* occurring.'

Drago nodded. 'So you're Sheriff Creed, the good-for-nothing varmint who wasted my time delivering nothing just so nothing much could happen. Or as they're saying about you – ninety per cent alcohol, ten per cent lawman.'

Creed gritted his teeth. 'Perhaps, but that'll change when this shipment gets through safely.'

'That'll be because of the diligence of my men and not because of any *help* from you.'

'Either way, it's in both our interests that everything goes well. Be obliged if we work together on that.'

Drago glared back then, with a deep sigh, provided a curt nod. He glanced at Jonah and snorted.

'This your deputy?'

Jonah bustled forward. 'I'm not a lawman. I'm Jonah Eckstein. You may remember me from last month's attempted—'

'I do. What's a clerk doing here?'

'I'm assisting Sheriff Creed and making available to him my expertise on—'

'I ain't interested.' Drago stabbed a finger at Jonah's chest, the slight blow knocking him back a pace. 'Just keep quiet. My men ain't got time to waste on you two and your ridiculous schemes. And I don't take kindly to people who irritate me.'

As Jonah mopped his brow, Creed brushed past Drago and vaulted into the carriage. He watched Jonah struggle up, then turned to look into the dark interior.

When his eyes became accustomed to the gloom, he saw that six wagon riders stood facing outwards from a small crate. Through the gaps in the slats, Creed could see four bags resting inside.

'Just as I told you,' Jonah whispered, then lowered his head when Drago swung into the carriage and glared at him.

'Like he says,' Creed snapped, 'is that all your protection, Drago?'

'I got enough men ensuring those bags stay here,' Drago muttered.

'And if someone just gets by them, they'll—'

'Someone won't just get by them,' Drago shouted, waving a firm finger in Creed's face. 'And a lawman who's offering advice like that in another lawman's county is going to irritate me.'

As the train whistled, then lurched to a start, each man glared at the other. Then Creed sauntered to the open door. Over the heads of the wagon riders, he watched the station fall back, then turned to face Drago.

'I ain't here to irritate you. I just have plenty of protection experience.'

'Only experience you have is being behind outlaws. I face them down.'

'Not always.'

'I've failed on the open trail when I've only had two men. This time, I have a secure carriage with twelve men, plus ten per cent of a lawman and some clerk.' Drago took a long pace to loom over Creed. 'And I reckon you've seen enough. Be obliged if you'd join the other passengers now.'

Creed stood his ground. 'We'll stay here.'

'You'll leave this carriage.' Drago glanced over Creed's shoulder at the plains, which hurtled by as the train built up its full speed. 'One way or the other.'

Creed glanced over his shoulder. He gulped.

'I'll sit in the passenger carriage.'

Drago chuckled, his men joining in the laughter.

With Jonah at his side and the wagon riders' laughter echoing in his ears, Creed strode through the carriage's side entrance. He tore his gaze from the sleepers speeding by beneath his feet and vaulted the gap to the passenger carriage.

He watched Jonah take a nervous glance at the track blurring by below, then take a long step over the gap. Creed smiled and walked inside.

As instructed, the porter had placed the strongbox by the first seat and Creed and Jonah sat on either side of it.

Jonah lifted the lid and removed its only contents, a shovel and a newspaper. He slipped the shovel beneath the seat then, with a snap of his hands, opened the paper and hid behind it.

Creed glared down the carriage.

The dozen or so occupants were all either conversing or looking out of the windows with the sullen boredom that all long journeys induced. But on the back seat, a man sat with his hat pulled over his eyes and both feet sprawled on the seat facing him.

For ten seconds Creed stared at the man, then the man tipped back his hat and winked.

CHAPTER 12

As the train rattled through the next two stations, Creed tapped his foot on the floor and bided his time.

At each stop, he pressed his face against the window and watched the wagon riders jump down from the carriage to secure the platform. While he watched their every move, Jonah hid behind his paper.

At last Creed's irritation got the better of him and he batted Jonah's paper from his grip.

'Getting to wonder why I brought you along,' he snapped.

Jonah shrugged. 'I've wondered that ever since we left Lincoln.'

'Then watch what's happening instead of reading that paper. You're here to uncover Drago's weaknesses.'

Creed glared at Jonah, then, with an angry snort, turned to stare out of the window.

Outside, Drago ordered two men to take up different positions, hurrying them on with colourful oath-filled commands.

'And what have you learned in your studious observations?' Jonah asked.

Creed glared through the window, watching until Drago disappeared from view back into the transportation carriage.

'I've studied Drago's procedures each time we've stopped.'

'I know you're doing that – as does Drago, the wagon riders, and everyone else in this carriage.'

Creed folded his arms and leaned back in his seat.

'As I intended. A lawman has to let everybody know that he's around.'

Jonah laughed. 'Are you always this subtle when you enforce the law?'

'Yup.'

'Explains a lot.'

'What you mean?'

'You ain't caught the Bell gang or the Ten Per Cent gang. And you won't unless you learn subtlety.'

'I am being subtle,' Creed muttered, flaring his eyes. 'You don't want to see me when I ain't.'

Jonah gulped. 'I don't, but you're watching the wagon riders to discover who amongst them is the weak link, but because they know you're watching them, they won't betray themselves.'

Creed leaned forward in his seat and pointed at the paper.

'And sitting behind that helps, does it?'

'It does.' Jonah shuffled the paper on his lap, then lifted it again, a grin emerging as his face disappeared.

With an outstretched finger, Creed lowered the paper.

'That smug grin tells me you reckon you know something.'

Jonah licked his lips as he lowered the paper to his lap and leaned to Creed.

'I have observed several interesting things subtly when you weren't showing everyone that you're a lawman. I know who your weak link is.' Jonah lowered his voice to a whisper. 'It's Drago.'

'Why?'

'Because he makes all the important decisions. If he ordered his men to throw the shipment out the door and put their hands over their eyes for ten minutes, they'd do it. With that sort of power, you can do anything.'

Creed sat back on his seat. 'Possibly.'

'And there's more. Someone on this train is in on the raid. At both the last two stops, a man has sauntered down the platform and glanced at Drago.'

'A glance doesn't mean anything.'

'Perhaps, but I reckon that if he didn't know that you were watching, he might have done something more.'

Creed frowned. He lowered his head a moment, then held out a hand.

'You got any of that paper I can borrow?'

Jonah peeled off two sheets and handed them to Creed.

'A few lessons in subtlety, and who knows, you might learn something.'

Creed shuffled the paper open and hid behind it.

'Don't want to learn anything from a toad like you,' he muttered.

In late morning, the train pulled up at Valance, the last stop before they entered Marren County.

Creed slipped off the train and strode to the waiting-room. He leaned against the wall and glared at Drago and the wagon riders, watching their movements.

Then he noticed Jonah in the carriage, hiding behind his paper, and nodded to himself.

He peeled from the wall and walked down the platform.

At the ticket-office, he stared at a notice-board, pretending to read, then, throwing out his legs with exaggerated kicks while stretching his back, strolled around the side of the waiting-room.

At the back, he was alone.

With a quick gesture, he glanced into the back of the waiting-room, confirming that it was empty, then slipped open the window. He rolled through the window and snaked across the floor to the front.

He located a knot hole in the wall and peered through. For long moments, he watched the wagon riders.

Just as the first flurries of irritation hit him for having taken Jonah's advice on subtlety, a fair-haired man stepped off the second train carriage.

The man glanced up and down the platform, then ambled along the side of the train. With a swift dart of his head, he glanced into the passenger carriage at Jonah, then continued past.

Jonah turned over a sheet, then hid behind his paper again.

The man wandered to the end of the platform. He turned, staring in all directions, then lifted on his heels twice and walked back down the platform.

As the man reached the second transportation carriage, he glanced inside, then sauntered past.

The wagon riders watched him leave with sullen disinterest.

At the second passenger carriage, the man jumped aboard.

Inside the waiting-room, Creed smiled to himself.

'Nathaniel McBain,' he whispered.

CHAPTER 13

Eight miles out of Valance, Creed edged closer to the window and peered outside.

A broken fence came into view, its haphazard line snaking across the plains. This fence marked the edge of a ranch long since abandoned, but Creed knew its significance.

With a tip of his hat to Jonah, he stood and wandered from the carriage.

The wagon rider guarding the door to the transportation carriage sneered at Creed, but with a short mocking bow, he let him enter.

Creed took a long pace into the carriage and tipped his hat to Drago. Drago looked up, shaking his head.

'Get out,' he muttered.

'You had a right to say that when I was out of my territory.' Creed raised his eyebrows. 'But we just passed over the county boundary. This is my territory and as the legally appointed—'

'Yeah, yeah. I understand. I suppose I could accept your help.' Drago licked his lips. 'I could do with ten per cent more assistance.'

Several men chuckled at Drago's humour, but Creed shrugged.

'I have one suggestion to make the shipment safer.' Creed leaned on the train wall. 'I'll need two of your strongest men to come with me.'

Drago glared back, then with a few brisk gestures ordered two men to go with Creed.

Five minutes later, the two men staggered back into the carriage, carrying the strongbox, Creed leading them with a fixed smile on his face.

The men manoeuvred the strongbox to the middle of the carriage. With a nod to each other, they dropped it for it to land with a huge thud.

Drago pushed from the wall and strode to the box. He kicked it, then looked up at Creed with his hands on his hips.

'And how will this tin box make the shipment safer?'

'It covers your only weak point.'

Drago backed from the box, shaking his head. He pointed at the men surrounding the shipment, then the men guarding the doors.

'I got a dozen men guarding a solid railway carriage. Nobody that I don't consider welcome gets in here. And you want to put the shipment in there to make it safer?'

'You got it. If you get any brighter, you could be a lawman.'

Drago pointed a firm finger at Creed.

'One more insult and Marren County will need a new lawman. I ain't putting anything in there. It's useless.'

'It's security, in case a raid gets past your solid walls and even more solid men.'

Drago rolled his head back to glance at his men and chuckled.

'Are you telling me you have a dozen more armed guards hiding in there?'

Drago's men laughed, but Creed bent down to pat a firm hand on the box.

'No. It's just covering your weak spot.' Creed pointed at the cash shipment in the crate. 'That crate is too portable. And if Bell raids us and gets away with the shipment—'

'Which won't happen.'

'*If* it happens, he faces this box. It's too sturdy to break into straight away and dynamite will destroy the cash. So he'll have to take it with him.'

'And how does that help?'

'It's heavy. It'll slow him down. I've had trouble catching Bell's gang because they're too fast. Loaded down with this, they won't be.'

Drago sneered. 'He'll still break into it.'

'He will, but it'll take time, and I'll use that time to catch him.'

Drago sauntered to the box. He circled it until he faced Creed.

'Your idea fails on one count – Bell won't get in here to get the shipment in the first place.'

'And if that happens, we'll both be happy. If it doesn't, this'll help. So we got nothing to argue about.'

For long moments Drago glared at Creed, then sighed.

'If I agree, will you stop annoying me?'

'Yup.'

'Then the shipment goes in your tin box.'

Creed provided his most pleasant smile.

'Obliged.'

'But the second we've left Marren County, it's coming out.'

'The second we leave Marren County, I couldn't care less what happens to the shipment.' Creed looked Drago up and down. 'You could steal it yourself and it wouldn't concern me.'

Drago narrowed his eyes, then turned and barked orders to two of his men. These men threw open the crate, extracted the bags, and dragged them to the box.

Creed swung the box lid open. He patted the sides, receiving a solid thud in return, placed each bag in a corner of the strongbox, then swung the lid closed. As the lid landed with a resounding slam, he extracted a large key from his pocket. He slipped it into the lock and turned his wrist, but the key refused to move.

He strained harder, but the key was still firm.

Drago chuckled. 'Seems like your tin box is a good idea, after all. If it's as hard to open as it is to close, nobody will ever get in it.'

With laughter peeling on all sides, Creed grabbed a projection on the side of the box and shook the whole box, only managing to lift the heavy box a few inches with each shake.

Inside, the bags thudded as they fell over. Creed lifted the box higher, straining with his one-handed effort while tugging on the key. Then, with a lunge, the box slipped from his grip and rattled to the floor.

But the key turned, the sudden movement rocking Creed to his knees.

'Ten per cent of a sheriff,' Drago said, chortling and slapping his thighs, 'but ninety per cent of an idiot. Now hand over the key and get out of my sight.'

Creed stood and righted his jacket, then wiped his warm cheeks. He slipped the key into his pocket.

'I'll keep it.'

Drago thrust out a large palm. 'You ain't. Give it to me.'

'The shipment is in Lincoln's bank box while it's in my county and so I'll guard the key.' Creed patted his pocket, then shrugged his jacket closed. 'When we leave my county you can have it back.'

Drago stormed forward a large pace, bunched a huge fist, and shook it in Creed's face.

'I'm guarding the shipment. Now give me the key or I'll pound you into pulp.'

'You wouldn't hit a lawman.'

Drago sneered, but he lowered his fist. He glanced away, then turned on his heel to slug Creed in the guts. Drago didn't follow through with the punch but even so, Creed staggered back, gulping air.

Creed righted himself, then strode back to square off to Drago.

'You just made a big mistake.'

Drago glanced around. 'Anybody here witness anything untoward happening?'

A chorus of nays came from all around Creed.

Creed bunched his fists. 'I didn't mean that. I

don't hide behind a star.'

'Then you just made an even bigger mistake.' Drago widened his eyes and leaned down to glare at Creed.

Creed shrugged. With his left hand, he tipped back his hat, then followed through, slapping Drago's cheek with the back of his hand.

As Drago's head rocked back, he slugged him deep in the guts with the other hand, then bundled him to the floor with shoulders and fists.

Drago skidded back across the floor and lay a moment. Then he rolled to his feet with greater ease than his size would suggest he could.

He stormed forward, bearing down on Creed with his fists raised.

Creed stood his ground and slammed another blow into Drago's guts, but with Drago prepared the blow merely slammed into muscle. Creed tried a combination of jabs and round-armed punches but Drago merely took them all, his face set in a snide grin.

Creed stopped for breath.

'You finished?' Drago said, leaning down.

'I just—'

Drago swung his fist, the great ham of his hand crunching into Creed's chin, cracking his head back.

Creed staggered back, only the wall saving him from tumbling to the floor. He pushed from the wall only to walk into another solid blow to the cheek that sent him reeling.

He lay, his jaw and cheek numb, then looked up to see a long kick slamming in to him. He lifted to roll from it, but it still thundered into his guts, turning his insides to water as he rolled.

Creed stopped his roll, lying face down, and thrust his arms down, but as he tried to rise, a stamp on the back slammed his face into the floor, grinding dirt into his cheeks. Flat on his belly, he tensed, expecting another blow, but nothing came.

For long seconds he lay, letting the buzzing in his ears recede, then rolled to his knees.

Drago stood over him, flexing his hand and staring at the knuckles.

'You've got a solid jaw, Sheriff.' Drago grinned. 'But I still reckon it'll break before my hand does. Give me the key.'

'In my county . . .'

Drago lunged down, grabbed Creed's collar, and dragged him to his feet.

Creed tried to lift his fists, but he was too numb to force his limbs to work.

'You like your county that much,' Drago muttered, 'you can see it closer to.'

With Creed's trailing feet brushing the floor, Drago dragged him towards the open door. Creed kicked back trying to gain purchase, but in two long strides they were at the door.

The wagon riders peeled back, leaving the doorway clear.

In a desperate lunge, Creed grabbed the side of the door, his act stopping Drago from dangling him outside. With one leg outside and the side of his body pressed against the side of the door, Creed hung on.

He glanced down. A few yards below, the ground hurtled by, the jagged stones a blur. The cold wind whipped into his face, spicing his senses.

'The key,' Drago grunted in his ear.

Creed released his grip on the door and lifted his hand to his pocket, then slammed his elbow into Drago's guts.

Drago merely edged him outside another foot.

'You throw me out,' Creed shouted, the wind blasting his words away, 'and you'll never get in the box.'

Drago glanced down at the stones hurtling by below.

'And that should comfort you as you lie all broken and torn by the track for the next few days.' Drago edged Creed another foot outside. 'The key!'

Creed struggled, but found no give in Drago's firm grip. He lunged for the train wall, but his fingers merely brushed it. With his feet dangling and no hope of finding purchase, he slumped, then edged his hand to his pocket to extract the key. He tossed it into the carriage.

Drago chuckled, then hurled Creed after the key.

Creed landed on his side and slid to a halt by the wall. He lay quietly as Drago grabbed the key and took it to the box.

Drago glared at Creed as with a short twist of the wrist, he turned the lock then threw the box lid open.

Creed staggered to his feet. 'This ain't over, Drago.'

Drago removed the bags and hurled them into the corner of the carriage. Two wagon riders rushed to them and placed them in the crate.

'It is for you,' Drago muttered. 'I don't care if this is your territory. If you come in here again, you'll leave flung sideways off the train.'

'What we doing with the box?' a wagon rider asked.

'Show Creed what will happen to him if he returns.'

The men who'd brought the box into the carriage dragged it towards the opening.

'Wait!' Creed shouted. 'That box ain't mine. It's the bank's.'

'Then just get it out my sight.' Drago jabbed a firm finger at Creed's chest. 'And that goes for you too.'

With two wagon riders carrying the box behind him, Creed shuffled from the transportation carriage.

Drago muttered a last oath, then slammed the door shut.

In the passenger carriage, Creed slumped into his seat. The wagon riders threw the strongbox to the floor and with a last sneer at Creed, swaggered back to their carriage.

Creed rubbed his chin, then his guts, then settled back in his seat.

Jonah stared at him over the top of his paper.

'Everything go according to plan, Sheriff?' he asked.

Creed stretched. He suppressed a wince by forcing a smile.

'Sure did,' he said.

CHAPTER 14

At the back of the first carriage, Deputy Fairborn watched Sheriff Creed return followed by the wagon riders with the strongbox. He waited until the wagon riders had left, then stood and turned.

While staring left and right through the windows at the passing plains, he walked casually from the carriage. He slipped his gun from its holster, secreted it beneath his jacket, then paced over the gap and wandered into the next carriage.

Half-way along the carriage, he stopped beside a seat occupied only by a fair-haired man and sat beside him.

The man glanced at Fairborn and shuffled away from him, but under his jacket Fairborn pressed the barrel of his gun against the man's chest.

The man flinched, but Fairborn pressed the gun deeper into his ribs.

'Howdy,' Fairborn whispered, 'Nathaniel McBain, ex-lawman, ex-bounty hunter, and now ex-outlaw.'

'You know my name,' Nat muttered while keeping

his gaze set forward, 'now what of it?'

'I've looked into your life and I know you. You were a lawman, but resigned because of the lousy pay. I can understand that. I'm Alan Fairborn, Marren County's deputy sheriff. And sometimes even I wonder if it's all worth it.'

From the corner of his eye, Nat glanced at Fairborn, then down at the bulge digging into his ribs.

'You clearly got problems, but they ain't my concern, so I'd be obliged if you'd holster that gun.'

'I ain't.' Fairborn dug the barrel in another inch. 'I've made understanding your life my concern. You took up with a lowlife, Spenser O'Connor, but you've done so much arguing that you're sick of your partnership, so you might be interested in the deal I'll offer you.'

Nat shuffled on his seat away from the gun.

'You've done plenty of *trying* to understand me.'

Fairborn leaned towards Nat's seat, digging the gun back in.

'I have. And you're thinking about ending your scheme before Spenser double-crosses you and takes all the money. Now might be the time to avoid that happening, Nathaniel.'

'You don't know me as well as you think you do. So I'd better introduce myself.' Nat held out his right hand. 'I answer to Nat.'

Fairborn glanced at the hand, then with a short sigh, edged his gun back an inch from Nat's ribs.

'Nat it is.'

Nat flexed his side. 'Obliged. But I believe in something even stronger than the law – a man's word. I had a deal with Spenser and I'll stick with it, no matter what.'

Fairborn snorted. 'He's a lowlife and always will be. You were a lawman. And you could be again.'

'I got no desire to be the kind of man that goes against his word. If Spenser turns on me, that's his problem and I'll deal with it.'

'If he turns on you, you'll be dead before you get that chance.'

'I'd sooner die as a man who keeps his word than save my life by breaking it.' Nat slipped down in his seat and swung both his feet on to the opposite seat. With deliberate slowness, he lifted a hand and pulled down his hat over his eyes. 'Now unless you got any reason to arrest me, I'd be obliged if you'd take that gun off me and let me get some rest.'

'I got all the reasons I need to keep a gun on you. I reckon you're planning to break the law.'

'For a man who claims to understand me, you've forgotten plenty. I ain't breaking the law.' Nat lifted his hat a mite and glanced at Fairborn. 'But I do have reason to believe that Clayton Bell will raid this train, and when he does, I'll recover whatever he steals.'

'You got plenty of information.' Fairborn withdrew his gun and holstered it. 'And plenty of intent.'

'Information ain't a crime and neither is intent.' Nat lowered his hat and folded his arms as he shuffled down deeper into his seat.

'They ain't, but I tell you this as a deputy sheriff to

an ex-deputy sheriff.' Fairborn turned in his seat and stared at Nat until he lifted his hat again. 'I'm watching you. If Clayton Bell raids this train, I'll stop him long before you do. You can join me and work on the right side of the law, but if you don't, I'll deal with you just like I'll deal with Bell.'

Fairborn glared at Nat a moment, then turned to rise, but Nat grabbed his arm and pulled him back into his seat.

'And as an ex-deputy sheriff to a deputy sheriff, I'll tell you this, I got no reason to see you hurt.'

'That sounds like a threat to me.'

'It ain't. You think you're clever finding me.' Nat nodded forward. 'But I'm way ahead of you, and way ahead of Sheriff Creed and that slimy bank clerk.'

Fairborn gulped, covering his momentary discomfiture with a short rub of his forehead.

'I don't care that you've seen us. Only thing that should be on your mind is that I've seen you.'

'Maybe. But it's a pity that that's the only thing on your mind.' Nat nodded his head back. 'Because I'm also way ahead of Bell's men in the next carriage.'

Fairborn winced, unable to hide his surprise.

'How many?' he murmured.

Nat produced a small smile. 'Just two men, Deke Pewter and Kyle Samuels. But just before you came in here, they wandered down the carriage to look in on you and your sheriff. Then one of them threw a kerchief out of the window. That was a signal.'

'Why you telling me this?'

Nat lifted his jacket to glance down at the gun on

his hip, then laid his jacket back down so that he left his gun exposed. He looked up at Fairborn and fixed him with a firm gaze.

'Because I don't want a lawman to die from what I'm doing. I want the money, but not if it means endangering men like you. That you can trust.'

Fairborn nodded. 'I believe you, but it still doesn't change the way I feel about you and what you're doing.'

'Never asked that it should.'

Fairborn glanced over his shoulder at the door to the next carriage.

'As you seem to know plenty about this raid, you going to tell me when you reckon it'll start?'

Outside, a gunshot blasted. Everyone around Fairborn and Nat gasped and jumped to their feet to peer through the windows.

'I'll let you guess,' Nat said.

Fairborn jumped to his feet. He pulled his gun, then peered left and right through the carriage windows. On the right, a snake of riders was galloping down an incline towards the tracks.

Fairborn glanced down at Nat who'd shuffled into his seat so that he was lying flat with his hat covering his face. Fairborn turned, then in irritation turned back and batted the hat from Nat's head.

Nat's exposed face was smiling.

'Settle down, Deputy,' he said. 'Ain't no use getting all flustered.'

'I have my duty.'

'Ignore it. Bell has too many men. They'll steal the cash shipment.' Nat yawned and stretched his arms, then settled down. 'But Spenser and me have a plan to get it back. Just leave us to do our work.'

'You may think you're doing good, but you're worse than Bell. At least he ain't got a conscience.' Fairborn sneered. 'You had one, except you sold it for ten per cent.'

Nat glanced away, gulping. He grabbed his hat from the floor and swung it on his head.

Fairborn snorted, then dashed for the carriage door. Outside, the raiders still hadn't blasted any more gunfire, but the line of riders was now matching the train's speed.

Fairborn threw open the carriage door. He edged through and closed the door. None of the raiders were visible so he jumped across the gap and threw open the door to the first passenger carriage.

Behind him, the door crashed open.

Fairborn turned to order the following man to stay where he was, but the man, Deke Pewter, lifted his gun and fired in an instant.

Fairborn ducked. Deke's shot winged past his shoulder into the carriage wall and, with only a moment to consider, Fairborn hurled himself across the gap at Deke to crash into his midriff. With his shoulder, he pinned Deke against the carriage wall and, with his left hand, grabbed Deke's gun hand and swung it up.

Deke tightened his grip, the spasm blasting lead into the carriage's overhanging roof. Splinters rained down on Fairborn's shoulders as he slammed the gun back against the wall and again a second time.

Still, Deke kept his grip on the gun and, with his feet set wide, inched the gun towards Fairborn's head.

Fairborn threw up his right hand too and pinned Deke's gun hand back, but with his chest exposed. Deke slugged him in the guts with a short-armed jab. The blow knocked Fairborn back a short pace, leaving enough room for Deke to stamp down on Fairborn's instep.

In an involuntary spasm, Fairborn released his grip on Deke's gun hand to receive a back-handed swipe to the cheek. Fairborn fell back, only the rail saving him from a drop to the speeding tracks below. Still, he folded over the rail, only able to hang on, the tracks whistling by mere feet below him.

A gunshot sounded and Fairborn winced, but he felt no pain, only hearing a scream and a thud beside him, then a hand pulled him back up from the rail. Fairborn threw his hand to his holster, but another hand grabbed his arm.

Fairborn looked up to face Nat. Deke was no longer there.

'Suppose I got to thank you,' Fairborn said.

'Just proving you were wrong,' Nat said, releasing his grip on Fairborn's arm. 'I ain't sold my conscience yet.'

'That mean you're ready to help defend the train?'

Nat hung his head a moment, then sighed.

'Yeah, like I said, I got no desire to see a lawman die, but if we fail, I'll get the cash back under my usual terms.'

With a nod to Nat, Fairborn jumped back over the gap and grabbed the ladder leading to the roof. He clambered up it, edged on to the roof, and lay flat. Five seconds later, Nat joined him.

Fairborn shuffled to the roof edge and glanced down at the raiders below, then glanced back at Nat.

'You want deputized?' he asked.

'Nope.' Nat glanced at Fairborn and smiled. 'But if you want to join me, I'll give you a share of my bounty.'

'No deal,' Fairborn snapped.

Nat lay beside Fairborn. 'Then what's your plan?'

'I reckon that—'

A gunshot blasted into the roof beside Fairborn's head, throwing splinters into his face. In self-preservation he rolled back, crashing into Nat, the action saving him from a second gunshot that cannoned into the roof where his head had just lain.

Nat glanced down the carriage roof. The second raider planted on the train, Kyle Samuels, had also climbed on to the roof and now stood ten paces in from the back of the next carriage. He'd planted his feet wide and held his gun in both hands as he steadied his aim.

From his lying position, Nat ripped off two rapid shots. Both winged past Kyle, but they forced him to duck. Nat fired a third shot. It was wild too, but Kyle dropped and lay spread-eagled on the rooftop.

Fairborn glanced at Nat then at Kyle. In a sudden decision, he jumped to his feet. In two long strides he reached the end of the carriage and vaulted the gap, landing lightly, then hurtled along the roof of the next carriage.

Kyle planted his elbows in a firm triangle and aimed up.

Fairborn dashed two more paces then threw himself down to skid across the rooftop. Kyle's shot whistled over his head, then he slid into Kyle, knocking his gun up as he fired again. With a clawing hand, Fairborn slammed Kyle's face into the rooftop and knocked his gun away, then rolled on top of him but, with a bucking of his back, Kyle pushed Fairborn off him.

Fairborn hurled a strong grip around Kyle's neck and held on. With neither man able to control their movements, both men rolled to the side. In two rolls, they reached the roof edge, but Fairborn planted a knee wide and stopped their roll with him sitting on Kyle's chest. He leaned back and thrust Kyle's shoulders down, pinning him to the roof.

Gunfire blasted nearby. Fairborn glanced up.

On the top of first passenger carriage, Nat was flat out and firing at another raider who'd reached the roof from the raiding party.

Fairborn turned from Nat's predicament and flexed his shoulders ready to slug Kyle's jaw.

With his eyes wild, Kyle glanced to the side – the roof edge was just inches away.

Fairborn released his grip to hit Kyle, but Kyle thrust up, aiming to bundle Fairborn from the roof. Fairborn had anticipated the move and he rolled the other way, Kyle only succeeding in rolling himself over the side. But with a trailing hand, Kyle grabbed

Fairborn's left leg and his weight dragged Fairborn to the edge.

On the smooth rounded roof, Fairborn floundered for purchase, but found none.

Inexorably, Kyle's weight pulled on Fairborn's legs as he slipped down the carriage side and inch by inch, Fairborn slid to the edge of the roof.

CHAPTER 15

In the first passenger carriage, Sheriff Creed had smashed windows on both sides of the carriage. He darted between the two sides, but the raiders stayed just far enough back so that he couldn't get a clear shot.

Since the first gunshot Jonah had cringed between the seats behind the strongbox.

Then Trent edged his horse in towards the second passenger carriage and leapt from the saddle, landing out of Creed's view.

Creed leaned through the broken window.

Trent had grabbed the ladder on the side of the carriage and clung on, his legs struggling for purchase on the smooth wall. He gained his footing and righted himself, then held out a hand, waiting for the next raider to attempt the leap.

Creed took careful aim at Trent and fired. The shot clattered feet wide, but in return a volley of gunshots from the nearest riders peppered the glass, sending shards cascading around him.

When Creed ventured outside again, the raiders had three spare horses – so at least three men had gained access to the train – and a separate group was hurtling by, heading for the transportation carriages.

Creed reloaded, then edged back down the carriage as he holstered his gun. He sat in the last seat, hunched his knees to his chin, and pulled his hat low, aping Jonah's petrified posture at the other end of the carriage.

A minute later the door flew open and Trent swaggered inside. He roved his twin guns back and forth.

Muted screams sounded as the other passengers cringed into their seats. On the back seat, Creed edged down further.

Two more raiders filed through, their guns held out.

'We ain't looking for trouble from anyone here,' Trent shouted. 'This ain't the time for anyone to be a hero. You all know what we want and we ain't looking for anything else.'

Creed peered out from under his hat, then slowly slipped to his feet as another man strode through the door.

Creed whirled his hand, his gun clearing leather, but in a lightning move, Trent swung round and clubbed his jaw to knock him back against the wall. Creed slid to the floor. He shook himself and jumped to his feet.

A gun was aimed at his head and behind the gun, Trent's grinning face peered at him.

'Now look what we have here,' Trent said. He whistled through his teeth and beckoned Bell to slip through the door. 'We have ourselves a sheriff.'

*

On the roof, Kyle's weight dragged Fairborn's feet, then ankles, then legs over the side of the train.

In desperation, Fairborn pushed to a sitting position and hammered his fist down on Kyle's hand, but Kyle tightened his grip, even throwing up his other hand to grab Fairborn's right leg.

Fairborn scrambled, seeking purchase, but Kyle's weight was speeding his descent.

He glanced up. Nat was dashing down the carriage roof, his assailant vanquished and his gun held out.

Nat blasted lead at Kyle and then blasted again, but it was only on the third shot that Kyle flinched and slumped, a redness spreading across his chest. His grip released and with a wild thrusting of his legs, Fairborn kicked him away for him to fall to the ground, then tumble away as the train hurtled down the track.

Fairborn threw himself round to lie flat on the roof, but with his legs dangling over the side of the carriage, he didn't have enough weight on top to save himself. His legs scrambled for purchase, but found none and in a sudden rush, Fairborn slid from the roof.

With a last desperate lunge, he grabbed the roof edge and his hand held, stopping his fall but crashing him into the side of the carriage. He threw up his left hand and held on.

In another bone-jarring thud, he slammed against the carriage side and swung out again.

Then Nat hurled himself to the carriage roof, his long slide halting above Fairborn, a firm hand closing on Fairborn's hand.

'You can't pull me up without dragging yourself over,' Fairborn shouted.

'I can't leave you hanging,' Nat shouted, gripping his hand more tightly.

'Just . . .'

A bullet cannoned into the carriage roof beside him. Fairborn glanced down to see two raiders galloping towards him.

In manic desperation, Fairborn threw up his other hand. Nat grabbed it and, with a scrambling, pulling effort, Nat dragged him up until Fairborn could lever a leg over the side, then roll on to the roof.

A last bullet from below ripped through trouser cloth, but then Fairborn pushed back from the edge.

Both men lay a moment, regaining their breath with long gasping wheezes.

'Whose idea was it to go on the roof?' Fairborn said.

Nat chuckled. 'That would be yours.'

Fairborn glanced over the edge of the roof at the mass of raiders, then edged back.

'Then I reckon it's time I thought of a better idea to defend this train.' Fairborn righted his jacket. 'Bell won't steal the shipment by getting one man at a time on to the train. He'll have to stop it. So that means we have to keep it going.'

Nat nodded. 'Agreed.'

With Fairborn leading, both men edged down the carriage roof. With their heads low, they concentrated on keeping their footing.

They vaulted the gap to the first passenger carriage. At the end of that carriage, Fairborn glanced down. Drago had shut the doors into his transportation carriage.

With a glance back at Nat, he backed three paces and charged at the gap to leap over it.

Nat leapt the gap and joined Fairborn. Doubled over they edged along the roof.

A gunshot ripped through the air beside Fairborn. He glanced around, but from the centre of the carriage, he couldn't see the flanking raiding party below.

Then a second shot blasted, this time sounding close enough to trim the hairs on the back of his neck.

With Nat, he darted his gaze in all directions, but the roof was clear and no matter where he looked, he couldn't see where the shooting came from.

Faced by Trent and Bell, Creed let his gun clatter to the floor, then lifted his hands to shoulder level.

'I ain't opposing you.'

Bell grabbed Creed's collar and dragged him away from Trent, then gestured for Trent to head down the carriage.

'You double-crossed me,' Bell muttered. 'That's worse.'

'You wouldn't kill a lawman.'

'People say you're only ten per cent of a lawman.' Bell raised his gun, his eyes widening.

'I got a good reason for you to keep me alive,' Creed whispered.

Bell glanced down the carriage. Trent was beside the front seats and glaring down at the strongbox and the cringing Jonah. Two other men peered through the front window at the transportation carriage.

'Tell me and I'll consider.'

Creed took a deep breath. 'I know which men in your gang work for the Ten Per Cent gang.'

'Who?'

Creed laughed, the sound flat. 'I'm looking straight down the barrel of your gun. That don't encourage me to tell you.'

Bell smiled with an arc of yellow teeth.

'Tell me and I'll let you live.'

'I ain't as stupid as you look. I'm not doing that.'

'Then the information dies with you.' Bell slammed the gun against Creed's temple.

'And you'll die too. Even if you break into the transportation carriage and escape with the cash, you won't keep it for long because some of your men are people you shouldn't trust. They'll turn on you.'

Bell shrugged and lowered his gun a mite.

'Either tell me or don't. Ain't much assurance I can offer you other than my word.'

Creed considered Bell's grin. He smiled.

'I got better assurance.' Creed lifted a hand and edged it to his jacket.

Bell narrowed his eyes as the hand disappeared into Creed's inside pocket. Then a slow inch at a time, Creed removed the hand. Bell tensed but the hand emerged with a sheet of paper clutched between two fingers.

Creed held out the paper for Bell to snatch it from him. Bell batted the paper open and glared down at the two names written there.

'And?'

'Those are the names of the two men in your gang who will double-cross you.' Creed licked his lips and sneered. 'Pity you can't read.'

Bell shrugged and raised his gun. 'I'll just find someone who can.'

'But can you trust him?' Creed smirked. 'If the man you ask to read it to you is one of those names, he'll lie.'

Bell rubbed his forehead and glanced down the carriage. The three raiders were all staring at him and awaiting instructions.

'What's your bargain, Sheriff?'

'If you escape with the shipment, whether you lose it or not, I'll see you later and read you those names.'

'Agreed,' Bell snapped. He holstered his gun, then with a thundering right cross, hammered Creed's jaw, slamming him back against the carriage wall.

Darkness closed on Creed.

Another gunshot blasted near Fairborn, the ricochet ripping splinters from the carriage roof into his right foot.

Fairborn threw himself flat, but Nat kicked him in the side, sending him tumbling.

He glared up at Nat, but another shot blasted just where he'd been lying. Fairborn glared at the hole the gunfire had made in the roof. Then, with his heart racing, he realized from where the gunfire was coming.

The wagon riders in the carriage below were firing up through the roof.

Fairborn and Nat shared a glance, an unspoken moment that debated whether they should stay and be quiet or whether they should run.

Lead hurtled through the roof six inches from Nat's foot. Wasting no more time, Nat dashed down the carriage.

Fairborn leapt to his feet and pounded after him. Lead hurtled through the roof at his feet, sending splinters into his heels as he charged, heedless of where his feet landed.

Both men hurtled to the carriage end, running full tilt, and over the next transportation carriage, then threw themselves from the roof to land on the fuel pile, burying themselves to their knees in chopped wood. They lay a moment regaining their breath.

Then, surrounded by the heaps of wood, both men clambered towards the engine. The raiders were still back at the passenger carriages, but even so, both men glanced over their shoulders frequently.

Fairborn reached the engine first to confront the train driver who aimed a rifle at his head.

'Git back, you varmints,' the driver muttered, his gun arm firm.

'We're here to help,' Fairborn said, raising his hands. 'I'm Deputy Fairborn and this is . . . a friend.'

The driver lowered his rifle and edged back to his engine.

'What d'you want?'

'We're here to defend the engine. We have to keep

it moving or the raiders—'

'Yeah, I know the routine. This ain't my first time.' The driver patted the engine. 'We've survived a few scrapes and we'll git you thro' this one too.'

Fairborn nodded and took a position at the right hand side of the engine. Nat stood on the left.

The driver snorted. 'You can poke your guns all y'like, but stoking wood will save y'life.'

Fairborn glanced down at wood heaped at the back of the engine and the shovel poking from the top.

'Nat, you stoke the wood,' he shouted. 'I'll head them off.'

Nat glanced back at Fairborn and shook his head.

'I got a better idea. You stoke and I'll defend.'

A gunshot skidded off the engine roof.

'You'd better decide who's doing what,' the driver shouted, 'or you won't git that chance.'

With an irritated shake of his head, Nat grabbed the shovel. He kicked the engine door open and hurled a shovel full of wood inside.

Fairborn watched him a moment, then peered from the engine.

The raiders were all two carriages back. He dashed to the other side. Again, the raiders were still concentrating on gaining access to the passenger carriages and ignoring the transportation carriage where the cash shipment was.

'Just as you should,' he whispered to himself.

CHAPTER 16

After ten minutes of furious shovelling, Nat stood tall and flexed his back.

'What's happening?' he shouted.

Fairborn leaned from the engine. 'Bell's raiders are leaving.'

Nat threw down his shovel, but Fairborn spun round and pushed him back.

'What you doing?' Nat snapped.

'You're doing a good job shovelling.' Fairborn pointed at the shovel. 'So you should carry on.'

'If the raiders have gone, I reckon we've failed to defend the train and I can stop helping you. I'm leaving.' Nat turned to the engine driver. 'Time you stopped this train.'

The driver glanced at Fairborn, who nodded and, with a pull on the brakes, the train wheels screeched as he slowed it.

'Even when we've stopped,' Fairborn said, '*you* are going nowhere.'

'You can't stop me,' Nat muttered.

'You wouldn't fight a lawman, Nat.' Fairborn raised his gun. 'So just stand there and be quiet. You ain't claiming your ten per cent recovery fee today. The lawmen are in control.'

With a sneer and a bat of his hand against his thigh, Nat sat on the wood pile.

'You ain't in control. Spenser and me know all Bell's hiding-places. If you want to see any of that money again, you'll let me go.'

Fairborn smiled as the train lurched to a halt.

'All right, Nat. I'll make a deal with you. If you can tell me what's happening outside, you can join Spenser. But if you're wrong, you come with me as a temporary deputy.'

Nat narrowed his eyes, then nodded.

'All right. Bell's gang is into the hills. They've split into four groups and are heading in different directions, some as decoys, one with the cash. They'll meet up later.'

Fairborn nodded. 'And the wagon riders?'

'They've reformed outside the train and are mounting their horses from the first carriage. Then they'll chase after Bell.'

'Will they catch him?'

'They'll fall back.' Nat smiled. 'When Bell's too quick for them. That's where Spenser and me come in.'

Fairborn shrugged and stood aside. 'Come on. Let's see how much of that is right.'

Nat rolled to his feet and edged past Fairborn. With a quick dart of his head, he glanced around the side of the engine. He shrugged, wandered to the other side of the engine and peered outside. He tipped back his hat to scratch his head, then turned back to Fairborn.

'Where are the wagon riders?'

'Drago ain't in pursuit. He's still in the transportation carriage.'

'What? But he should be . . .'

Fairborn allowed a full smile to break out.

'Nat, it's time for you to accept that you're no longer in control. The lawmen are.'

Fairborn jumped down from the engine. With Nat at his side, he walked down the side of the train. He glanced up at the closed doors of the transportation carriage, then sauntered past to the first passenger carriage.

Several passengers had already emerged from the train and had huddled in animated groups, discussing what had just happened and swapping tales.

Fairborn tipped his hat to one group, then levered himself on to the train. Nat followed.

Fairborn wandered into the carriage. Creed was standing at the back of the carriage, probing his jaw. He smiled and tipped his hat.

'Fairborn.'

'Creed.' Fairborn stood aside.

'And you're Nathaniel McBain.' Creed widened his smile and beckoned Nat to follow him down the carriage.

Nat shrugged. 'I answer to Nat.'

Nat followed Creed to the last seat, where Jonah was cringing on the floor. The strongbox had gone.

Creed offered Jonah his hand.

Jonah glanced at Nat, then gulped and grabbed

Creed's hand, his fingers shaking with an uncontrollable tremor.

'Don't ever get me into that kind of exploit again,' he croaked, then cleared his throat. 'I thought those outlaws would kill me. That was the worst thing that's ever happened to me.'

Creed pulled him to his feet. 'I had my doubts that you were the right man to bring along. But I was wrong. You look just scared enough to be plausible.'

Jonah extracted a kerchief and blotted his sweating cheeks and brow.

'That's because I was scared.' He glanced down at his shaking hand. 'Still am for that matter.'

Creed shrugged and brushed past him.

'Come on,' he said. 'We got some people to deputize.'

The four men paced from the carriage and into the transportation car.

Inside, Drago was pacing back and forth.

'Bell only stole your tin box,' he shouted.

Creed shrugged. 'He did, but that box was bank property. I'd be obliged if you'd help me get it back.'

Drago snorted. 'That ain't my concern. As Bell stole it in your county, I reckon you should chase after it. We'll stay here and guard our shipment.'

Creed glanced at Fairborn and winked.

Fairborn returned the wink.

Creed sauntered to the door and patted the spot where'd he hung on only thirty minutes earlier. He paced back to stand before Drago.

'It's a pity that you won't help me. The strongbox is well worth recovering. A master metalworker constructed it using classical dimensions.' Creed held his arms wide, signifying each measurement. 'Five foot long, four foot high and three foot wide.'

'If he's kept the plans,' Drago snapped, 'perhaps he can make you another one.'

'Perhaps he could, but it won't be as good as the original. You don't get many boxes that are four feet high.' Creed grinned and lifted on his heels to get the smallest of height advantages on Drago. 'But only two foot six inches deep.'

'What's that mean?' Drago snapped.

'It means that the box was eighteen inches bigger on the outside than it appeared to be on the inside because a false bottom topped the lowest eighteen inches. And that false bottom pivoted when someone locked the box.' Creed held his hands out flat, then turned them over. 'An action that moved the contents that were under the false bottom to the top.'

For long moments Drago glared at Creed, then winced and rubbed his eyes.

'You mean that you switched the money?'

'Sure did. Like I said, I wanted to guard the cash in my county, and I decided to do that in the carriage outside.' Creed slapped his palm against his forehead. 'But I forgot that the metal worker who made the strongbox might not have been reliable. He might have talked about it to the wrong people, such as Clayton Bell.'

Drago stormed to the back of the train and crunched the toe of his boot against the crate containing the guarded bags.

'You telling me these bags are full of nothing?'

'Forged bills actually.'

With a great roar, Drago kicked the crate open, then grabbed a bag and hurled it against the wall.

'Be careful,' Creed said, stepping forward. 'Forged bills can fetch as much as a cent in the dollar and with fifty thousand of them in there, that's a few hundred dollars' worth.'

'You idiot!' Drago roared. He turned to Creed with his eyes blazing and his fists clenched. 'My men risked their lives guarding nothing while you lost the real cash out there.'

'That ain't how it is. Just like all your past failures, you were planning to let Bell's raid succeed in return for a healthy pay-off.'

Drago advanced a long pace to loom over Creed.

'That's a brave claim when you're surrounded by my men.'

'It is, but you have one chance to rectify this. Work for me and get back the cash.' Creed glanced at Nat. 'And all for no fee.'

'We're having no part of this,' Drago snapped.

'You will.' Creed strode forward to stand toe to toe with Drago. 'A corrupt varmint like you will have charges to face, and he'll face them if he doesn't do as I say.'

Drago glared down at Creed. 'You can't threaten me. You've just broken enough laws to swing.'

'Perhaps, but I know how to avoid any of us facing that sort of trouble.' Creed took a deep breath and let the biggest smile for months emerge. 'Because I'm way ahead of you, way ahead of Nat, way ahead of

Spenser O'Connor, and way ahead of Clayton Bell and his gang. I'm in control.'

Drago lowered his head and slumped, his fists unclenching.

'What's your deal?' he whispered.

'You get deputized.' Creed pointed to Drago, Nat, then the rest of the wagon riders. 'We track down the cash and return with it and Clayton Bell in tow.'

'And no charges?'

Creed nodded and for long moments, Drago glared at him. Then he gave the shortest of nods, but behind him the wagon riders glanced at each other, then one at a time peeled from their positions to stand together.

'That goes for you too,' Creed said, still staring at Drago.

The nearest wagon rider snorted. 'We're having no part of this. We'll risk our lives to do our job, but we ain't risking ourselves to save Drago's hide. You have nothing on any of us.'

Drago glared over his shoulder at the line of wagon riders, then shook his head.

'Go on, if you ain't man enough to join me.'

'Reckon as we ain't. We'll enjoy the rest of the journey from the comfort of a real seat.'

One by one, the wagon riders filed out of the transportation carriage. Creed watched them go, then turned to the scowling Drago and Nat.

'Looks like it's just us, then.'

Nat snorted. 'You just crossed the line, Sheriff. You hate my version of vigilantism, but what you've just done was far worse than anything I've done.'

'Ain't looking for your approval.' Creed patted Fairborn's shoulder. 'Reckon as you ought to start smiling like Fairborn is.'

Fairborn widened his smile, but Nat glared at him, shaking his head.

'Deputy,' Nat muttered, 'you just sold your conscience for a far cheaper price than I did.'

Fairborn met Nat's firm gaze a moment, then lowered his head.

CHAPTER 17

Standing outside the train, Deputy Fairborn watched Sheriff Creed commandeer horses from the transportation carriage. Then, with his reluctant new deputies at his side, Creed rode after Bell's gang, leaving Fairborn and the even more reluctant Jonah Eckstein behind.

'Can I go now?' Jonah whined.

'You got one more job to help me with.' Fairborn patted Jonah's shoulder. 'But cheer up. At least this job won't involve gunfire.'

Jonah smiled. 'At least that. What do you want me to do?'

'Get me a horse, and unload one for yourself before the train leaves.'

Jonah nodded and grinned hopefully. 'And when you've gone, can I go back to Lincoln?'

'Nope. You're waiting for me here. Then you'll help me track down Bell.' Fairborn leaned down and smirked. 'And I reckon there'll be plenty of gunfire then.'

'I was afraid you'd say that.'

Jonah mopped his brow, then bustled along the side of the train.

Fairborn watched Jonah roll into the first carriage, then leapt into the empty transportation carriage. Scattered about the carriage were the money bags.

He smiled and kicked a bag.

'People can be such idiots,' he whispered to himself.

Sheriff Creed and his new deputies galloped along the trail, but they saw no signs of Bell's gang other than the lines of hoof-prints, which hurtled off in all directions. They followed the tracks with the cart-wheel ruts.

Five miles on, they approached the mesa, scene of their failed trap the previous month. Creed directed the group from the trail and away from the tracks.

Nobody questioned his orders.

They headed up a gully to reach the top of the mesa, then rode across the rocky plateau and down through another long gully, emerging on to the plains where, to Creed's directions, they headed to the east of Lincoln.

As there were no obvious tracks for Creed to follow, Nat and Drago shared a glance, then followed him.

Another hour of riding later they approached Turner Galley's smithy, ten miles out of Lincoln. Creed allowed himself a smile – a line of horses bustled in a corral at the back.

Drago snorted. 'How did you know Bell would be here?'

Creed tipped back his hat, his smile growing.

'Like I said, I'm way ahead of everyone.'

A hundred yards back from the smithy, the men halted their horses and tethered them to a tree. Then, running doubled over, they snaked towards a rock pile set before the building.

They were ten yards away when a burst of gunfire blasted into the ground before them and the three men speeded, then hurled themselves head first behind the rocks.

Creed batted dust from his jacket and leaned back against a rock.

'You three fine?' he asked.

'Yeah,' Nat muttered. 'We're just waiting to see what you want us to do next. Seeing as how you're way ahead of everyone.'

Creed nodded and lifted his head a fraction above the rock.

'We've found you, Clayton Bell,' he shouted. He waited a moment for a reply that didn't come. He raised his voice. 'I said, we've found you, Bell.'

'You don't have many men out there,' Bell shouted through the smithy's only window, his head appearing for a moment before he stood to the window's side.

Creed snorted. 'Don't need many men to take down your type. Come out and hand over the money.'

'We ain't coming out to your orders, Sheriff. We'll come out when we choose to. If you want to live, you'd better not be here when we do.'

'You won't kill me. I'm your only chance of living.'

Creed laughed. 'Unless you've learned to read real quick.'

Bell snorted and slammed the shutters closed.

'What did that mean?' Drago asked.

'Like I've been telling you.' Creed leaned back against the rock and checked his gun was fully loaded, then looked up, smiling. 'I'm in control of this situation. I'm way ahead of everyone here.'

'As you keep telling us,' Drago snapped. 'So what do we do now?'

'We wait for fifteen minutes, then the in-fighting in Bell's gang starts. When the gunfire has reduced their numbers, we'll move in.'

'How do you know . . .'

Nat patted Drago's shoulder and sighed.

'Like the sheriff said,' Nat murmured, 'he's way ahead of everyone here.'

Inside the smithy, Clayton Bell strode from the window to the bench where Turner Galley was still working on the strongbox's lock.

'Why ain't you in there?' Bell muttered.

Turner looked up and wiped a layer of sweat from his brow.

'I'm going as fast as I can. That idiot sheriff broke the key off in the lock.'

'How much longer?'

'Ten minutes.'

'You said it'd be ten minutes, twenty minutes ago.'

'And it'll still be ten minutes in another twenty minutes if you keep talking to me.' Turner gulped at his sudden defiance and hunched over the strongbox.

Bell pulled his gun and aimed it at the lock.

'Reckon I know a quicker way.'

'Don't,' Turner shouted, lifting a hand. 'I've seen people try to do that and shoot themselves with a ricochet. This is solid iron. You ain't ever shooting your way in here. I built this to last.'

Bell slammed a solid hand on Turner's shoulder. Turner flinched.

'Telling me about this box persuaded me not to kill you last month. Getting into it will prove I shouldn't change my mind.'

'I built this.' Turner peered into the lock. 'I'll dismantle it.'

Bell glared at Turner, then sauntered to the pile of branding-irons. He lifted the topmost.

'You have ten minutes, then I find a use for these.'

Turner looked up and laughed, the sound hollow.

'You're just like that Sheriff Creed. He threatened to brand me with that big T too.' Turner leaned over the box and poked at the lock. 'He said he was going to brand my name on me.'

Bell glanced at the brand, then moved over to the wall, tapping the iron against his thigh.

Trent joined him. 'What did Creed mean about him being the only one who could save you?'

Slim and Dave glanced up, but Bell glared at them until they looked away, then shifted to the corner of the smithy out of their hearing range.

'Inside the train I could have killed Creed,' he whispered, 'but I didn't when he bargained for his life.'

'What did he offer?'

'He'd been investigating.' Bell lowered his voice to the lowest of whispers. 'He'd found the names of the two people in here who are working for the Ten Per Cent gang. He wrote down their names, guessing I wouldn't trust anyone enough to let them read the names to me.'

Trent glanced around the room, looking at Fletcher, who stood at the window and Dave, who stood by Turner, then across at the rest. He sighed.

'You can trust me to read them to you.'

'I know.' Bell rubbed his brow, staring at the strongbox. 'But you get to thinking.'

With a steady whistle, Trent breathed slowly through his nostrils, then nodded.

For long moments, Bell stared at Turner as he worked on the box. Then he reached into his pocket and with the paper clutched between two fingers, passed it to Trent.

Trent grunted an acknowledgement, then opened the paper and read the names. His eyes narrowed.

'Our traitors are Carlos Pitcairn and . . .' Trent took a deep breath and lowered his voice to the lowest of whispers. 'And Hardy Newman.'

'Both dead.' Bell sneered. 'That sheriff must have been playing a trick by picking the dead ones.'

'He wouldn't know they were dead. Besides, they were the biggest troublemakers we had. They were my prime candidates too.'

Bell nodded. 'So we have nothing to worry about. Nobody in here will turn against us.'

'Seems that way.'

Trent crunched the paper into a ball and opened

his hand. He flexed his fingers as the paper fell to the floor, them strolled across the room to join Fletcher at the window.

Bell glanced at the sweating Turner, who now seemed to be using every tool in his workshop to get into the strongbox. He kicked the screwed-up paper at the wall and sauntered three paces towards the strongbox, tapping the brand against his leg.

Turner glanced up, then grabbed the largest of his hammers and began an insistent tapping on the lock.

'Branding Turner's name into his hide using this brand,' Bell whispered to himself. He lifted the brand and stared at the two connected lengths of iron. He traced a finger across the brand, mouthing to himself.

With a last glance at the window, where Trent was staring outside, he edged back to the crunched-up paper and grabbed it. He opened it and pressed it flat.

Four blocks of shapes were on the paper. The first two blocks were just a meaningless jumble to Bell, but the third block started with the same shape as the branding iron.

Bell traced his finger along the letters and found the same shape at the end.

'One of the traitor's names starts with a T and ends with a T.' Bell stabbed at his brow as he forced his mind to consider his limited knowledge of lettering. He mouthed the 'T' sound to himself. 'And that ain't Hardy or Carlos.'

He glanced at Turner, mouthing Turner's name.

The brand dropped from his slack fingers and

clattered to the floor.

Turner glanced up, then returned to hammering the box.

Dave wandered over to him. 'What's up, boss?'

'I know who the traitors in our gang are,' he whispered.

Dave gulped and backed a pace. 'Who?'

'Carlos was one.' Bell took a deep breath. 'The other is Trent.'

'Trent,' Dave muttered. He glanced over his shoulder at the window.

'Yeah, Trent,' Bell roared. 'Trent's the traitor. Kill him!'

From across the plains, Deputy Fairborn and Jonah Eckstein rode to the smithy. Fairborn dismounted at the tree where Creed and the other had tethered their horses, then dashed to Creed's position with Jonah's smaller form waddling at his side.

Inside the smithy, sporadic gunfire was echoing.

'Plenty of shooting going on,' Fairborn said, flopping down beside Creed.

Creed smiled. 'Yeah, and all of it's inside the smithy and none of it's aimed at us.'

'What's happening?'

Drago snorted. 'As Creed keeps telling us – everyone is just following his plan.'

Creed chuckled. 'They sure are. Bell's just figured out that his gunslinger is one of the traitors in the gang.'

As Nat glanced at Creed, his brow furrowed, Fairborn frowned.

'But Dave Gordon and Slim Johnson are the ex-members of Kirk Morton's gang, not Trent. As far as I could tell, he's loyal.'

Creed glanced at Drago, the smile that he'd sported for the last hour turning into a grin.

'I got me a talent for switching bags, and it seems I got me the same talent for switching names.'

'You mean you lied?' Drago said.

'Nope. I sowed a seed and let Bell's twisted mind sprout it into something that'll help us.'

A gunshot blasted into the rocks before them and all five men ducked.

'Seems that your plans didn't finish them all off,' Nat said.

'But with their gunslinger gone, the odds are better. So now it's time to finish a job that's become a whole lot easier.' Creed glanced at each man in turn, receiving nods, but when he glanced at Jonah, the small man was cowering on the ground with his hands clutched over his ears. 'What's wrong, toad?'

Jonah peered up from under his arms.

'All this shooting,' he whined.

'But this is the sort of trouble you cause when you sell information to outlaws. Thought you'd appreciate seeing it first hand.'

'I don't,' Jonah whimpered.

'Want a gun to help us sort this out?'

'No. I've never owned a gun. I'd probably just shoot off my own foot.'

'So you'd prefer to let one of Bell's gang shoot you instead, would you?'

'Quit mocking me. I've followed you like you

wanted me to do. I helped you on the train, but this is too much.' Jonah glared up at Creed, his eyes wide and pleading. 'I ain't no use to you here today.'

'You ain't no use to anyone anywhere at any time, toad.'

Jonah placed the palms of his hands together and held out his hands, beseeching Creed to relent.

'Please let me go,' he whined.

'You're staying.' Creed peered down at Jonah, causing the small man to cower even further behind his rock cover. 'I'm handing out real justice today and you're another recipient. Every time a toad like you takes a bribe or sells information, another man suffers, usually at the end of a gun. I'm just letting you know what being that other man feels like. Then when someone next offers you a bribe . . .'

Creed leaned down and grabbed Jonah's collar. He dragged him up until his head was just below the cover.

'Please,' Jonah whined, 'I want to go.'

'One inch higher and somebody in Bell's gang will see you and they'll start shooting. You want a gun to defend yourself?'

'No, I just want to go. Please, please . . .' Jonah's voice died with a croaked whimper. Tears welled from his pleading eyes.

With an angry snort, Creed threw him to the ground.

'You ain't any kind of man. You're barely worth calling a toad.'

'I know, but . . .' Jonah sobbed. The tears cascaded down his cheeks and dripped to the ground.

Creed sneered. 'Go.'

Creed had just finished the word when Jonah leapt to his feet. With his small legs whirring and his head down, Jonas scampered away from the smithy, then arced to the trail and scurried for Lincoln.

'Hey, toad,' Creed shouted after him. 'Don't forget your horse. Lincoln is ten miles away.'

Jonah pushed his head down further, his scrambled gait suggesting that nobody would stop him now that he had the open plains and safety to head for.

Creed watched him a moment, then glanced around. The other three men were watching him leave. Nat and Fairborn were shaking their heads and smiling. Drago was sneering.

'Come on,' Creed said. 'Let's see if we can sort this out even without Jonah's help.'

All four men chuckled and rolled on to their fronts.

For an hour, Creed and his deputies waited for Bell to make his move, but aside from the occasional burst of gunfire from the window, all of which ripped into their rock cover, everyone remained in the smithy.

Twice, Bell fired at them, but Trent never appeared.

Then Creed glanced to the side into the plains. He narrowed his eyes, then turned to Nat.

'It's time you decided where your loyalties lie,' he muttered.

'I've already done that when you deputized me,' Nat said. 'When I give my word, I stick with it.'

'I believe you do, but what happens when you've

given your word twice and they're in conflict?' Creed pointed to the side.

A half-mile down the trail, a lone rider had stopped. He was too far away to recognize, but with his eyes narrowed Nat peered at him, then lowered his head a moment.

'Who is it?' Fairborn asked Creed.

'That's Nat's partner, Spenser O'Connor. He's finally realized that the trap they'd set for Bell didn't spring and now he's followed the trails here. He'll try his own raid on Bell, siding with Dave and Slim, if they're still alive.' Creed patted Nat's shoulder. 'So, are you still with him?'

Nat shook his head. 'I'm an honest man, so I'll tell you this. I'll try to help you capture Bell and the cash, as I promised, but I ain't stopping Spenser if he gets to the money first.'

Creed nodded and leaned his gun on top of his rock cover.

'Reckon that's the best I could have hoped for.'

CHAPTER 18

Fifty yards to the lawmen's right, Spenser O'Connor dismounted and leapt behind the only rock on that side of the smithy.

Creed watched him a moment, then turned to Drago.

'Drago,' he said, 'you're with me. We'll frighten off Bell's horses. Fairborn and Nat will cover us. Then we force Bell out.'

The group shared nods. Then Fairborn slammed his gun on the top of the rock and blasted at the window.

Fairborn's lead peppered the wall around the window as, with their heads down, Creed and Drago dashed for the corral at the side of the smithy.

While Fairborn reloaded, Nat blasted the window at a steady rate. Every time Fletcher poked his gun through the window, Nat fired again, forcing him to dart back inside.

With the covering fire stopping the men in the smithy returning fire, Creed and Drago reached the corral fence. On his belly, Drago snaked to the gate and edged it open, then shuffled back to join Creed.

The two men leapt into the only cover, a rain-washed gully, then slammed their guns on the side and joined Nat and Fairborn in firing, but they blasted over the heads of the horses in the corral.

The horses whinnied and bundled against the fences. One horse tried to leap the fence but crashed against it. The fence held, but another horse found the open gate and within moments it was free.

Then the other horses trailed outside after the free horse and galloped away, tossing their heads as they captured their freedom. Creed and Drago fired over their backs, encouraging them to gallop further away.

Thirty yards away, Nat edged to the side behind his cover to kneel closer to Fairborn.

'I reckon Creed's trusting me and Drago now,' he said.

Fairborn shrugged. 'Only just.'

'And do you trust me?'

'I trust you,' Fairborn said. 'I don't reckon you'll harm me after you saved my life back on the train.'

'I did do that, at least twice.' Nat glanced away then, with a short-armed jab, slugged Fairborn's jaw. The blow rocked the deputy's head back against the rock and he slumped to the ground, his head lolling. 'And I've just done it again.'

Nat slipped down behind his cover and pulled Fairborn to a sitting posture, leaning him against the rock in a position that ensured the people in the smithy wouldn't be able to see him.

In the gully, Creed edged up. He placed his hands

around his mouth and faced the rock behind which Spenser was hiding.

'Hey, Spenser,' he hollered, 'you were slow getting here.'

Spenser glanced up, then ducked. 'You know me by name. What of it?'

'I'm just showing you that I'm way ahead of everybody here. Now unless you want deputized like your partner, Nat, you'd better leave. You won't get a recovery fee today.'

'You're wrong, Sheriff. I'll get in there and reclaim the money.'

'You won't. Bell's killed your contacts in his gang. Your chances died as soon as Bell found out that Trent and Carlos were double-crossing him.'

Spenser glared back, his brow furrowed, then dashed for the smithy.

At the window, Fletcher arced a rifle barrel towards Spenser.

Creed considered a moment, then blasted at the smithy window, forcing Fletcher to fall back inside.

Spenser reached the smithy wall and pressed his back to it. He regained his breath, then edged along the wall towards the door.

He flexed his shoulders, then spun round to face the door. With a solid blow, he kicked the door open, then leapt to the side as gunfire exploded from inside.

Spenser stood a moment. Then, when the first volley of gunfire ended, he leapt inside through the open door, keeping low and skidding on his stomach across the timbers.

Inside, only six men were still alive. The bodies of the other men were draped over chairs or hunched in corners.

Dave was struggling with Bell, and Spenser's other contact, Slim, had turned on Fletcher.

The other two men swivelled at the hip, swinging their guns towards Spenser, but, from the floor, Spenser blasted up, ripping an arc of lead through the two men's stomachs.

As the two men fell away, clutching their guts, Spenser rolled to the side and leapt to his feet.

Spenser trained his gun on Slim's fight with Fletcher.

He watched Fletcher punch Slim to the jaw, sending him reeling. Spenser blasted lead at Fletcher, but Fletcher leapt behind a table, Spenser's last slug ripping past Fletcher's head and into the wall.

Bell and Dave still rocked back and forth as they struggled. But with a combination of shoulders and arms, Bell bundled Dave away from him, then ripped his gun from its holster and blasted him in the guts at short range.

Dave folded and collapsed to the knees only to receive a second blast to the forehead that spun him on to his front.

Spenser had just enough time to order Slim to take Fletcher. Then he charged Bell and pushed him back against the wall, levering his gun arm up as he slammed him back a second time.

With their feet set wide, both men struggled over Bell's gun.

Behind Spenser, Creed and Drago charged into the smithy.

Gunfire rattled as Creed blasted lead three times into Slim's chest, wheeling him over a bench.

Fletcher stayed down a moment. Then, with a great roar, he leapt to his feet. But he only had time to spray one wild shot over Creed's head before Drago slammed lead into his shoulder, spinning him round, then a second slug into his back that flattened him.

For long moments, Drago and Creed stood two paces in from the doorway, roving their guns back and forth as they dared more opposition to appear.

With his hands held high and a branding-iron held aloft in his right hand, Turner stood from behind the bench with the strongbox. Creed glared at him a moment, but as Turner thrust his hands even higher, he nodded.

Ten seconds later, Nat charged into the smithy to find that aside from Bell's and Spenser's fight, the battle was over.

Spenser gritted his teeth and ignored the silence that had descended behind him. He repeatedly slammed Bell's gun hand against the wall until the gun squirmed from Bell's hand.

Spenser ripped himself from Bell's clutches and lunged for the tumbling gun, but, finding himself momentarily free, Bell slugged Spenser's jaw, knocking him back and to the floor.

Bell fell to his knees and groped for his gun, but Turner dashed three long paces and crashed his branding-iron down squarely on Bell's head.

Without making a sound, Bell crumpled and lay still.

'Seems you've decided where your loyalties lie, Turner,' Creed said.

Turner grinned and patted the branding-iron.

'Yeah,' he said, 'with the winning side.'

'Drago,' Creed muttered, 'it's time for you to decide as well.'

'Done that already,' Drago said.

'In that case, guard Bell.' Creed glanced at the sprawling Spenser. 'And that failed outlaw.'

Drago strode two paces to stand over Spenser and ripped Spenser's gun from its holster. He hurled it away, then stood with his legs planted wide.

'What about Nat?' he asked.

Creed turned to face Nat. 'What about you? Are you still with us?'

Nat raised his hands to chest level. 'I ain't opposing you.'

Creed glanced through the open door, then narrowed his eyes.

'Where's Fairborn?'

'He's outside. A bullet winged him, but he'll be fine.'

Creed nodded and faced Turner. 'Thought you'd have unlocked that strongbox by now.'

'I built this to last.' Turner dropped his branding-iron and sauntered to his bench to pat the strongbox. 'And I figured that getting into this box was all that was keeping me alive.'

With a short twist of the wrist, Turner clinked the lock for the lid to fly open, then twisted a projection on the side.

The false bottom crunched as it turned.

'Bags still there?' Creed asked.

Turner peered inside, then nodded and stood to the side.

With his grin now threatening to split his face in two, Creed strode to the box and glanced inside.

A muffled cry and a scuffle sounded behind him. Creed swirled round.

Spenser had leapt to his feet and was struggling with Drago, each man locking his hands on the other's arms. Creed ignored their fight and turned his gun on Nat, forcing Nat to raise his hands high above his head and back a pace.

Drago wrestled Spenser to the side and, as Spenser tottered free, he punched Spenser deep in the guts.

Spenser sprawled back against the wall, clutching his guts, then rebounded and staggered forward, his arms out, his gait uncoordinated. Drago grabbed his right arm, pulled him around to face him, then rolled his shoulders and slugged his jaw with a long round-armed uppercut.

Spenser's feet left the floor before he slammed down on his back and slid ten feet, only halting when he ploughed into Slim's body.

Spenser lay a moment, then pushed up, his arms shaking.

'You can stay down, or you can get up,' Drago shouted. He cracked his knuckles. 'If I were you, I'd stay down.'

Spenser hung his head. Then he feinted to rise, but instead scrambled across Slim's body and levered a gun from his holster.

Drago scrambled for his gun, but in the fighting it'd fallen from him. He raised his hands.

'No more orders, Drago,' Spenser muttered. He turned the gun with a quick snap of the wrist on Creed. 'Same goes for you, Sheriff.'

Creed leapt behind the bench. He lay a moment, then rolled to his knees and rested his gun beside the side of the bench.

'You just made your final mistake, Spenser.'

'I ain't aiming to shoot you,' Spenser said. 'I just want the cash.'

From his covered position, Creed glanced at Nat.

'You got anything to add, Deputy Nat McBain?'

Nat shook his head. 'I ain't been a deputy for nigh on six months.'

With a short lunge, Nat lowered his hands and ripped his gun from its holster. He aimed the gun down at Creed.

On one knee, Creed swung his gun towards Nat, then stopped its motion and hung his head.

'That's two people who've made a final mistake.'

Nat gestured with his gun and Creed stood, keeping his gun held high.

To Nat's direction, Creed holstered his gun and backed to the wall to join Turner. Spenser directed Drago to join them.

With his gun held out, Nat stalked to the box. He removed the four strung-together bags, looped them over his shoulder, and backed to the door.

'Don't try anything heroic, Sheriff,' Nat muttered. 'We got what we came for.'

'Stop there, Nat,' Creed muttered. 'You can still

back off from this. You got tempted, but I'm prepared to overlook that for the good you did in helping to arrest Bell.'

'I'm just taking what I deserve for my hard work.'

'You can't steal money at gunpoint from a lawman and claim it's a recovery fee. For a crime like that, you know what you're facing.'

'And you created this situation. I got enough on your actions for you to know what you're facing.'

'I'm a lawman. I have nothing to fear. But you have everything to worry about. So now you have a decision to make.' Creed narrowed his eyes. 'Make the right one.'

CHAPTER 19

Nat glanced at Spenser, then Creed. He shrugged.

'Throw your gunbelt down, Sheriff, and kick it to me. Same goes for you, Drago.'

Creed snorted, but he unhooked his gunbelt and kicked it across the floor. Drago unhooked his belt and hurled it to Nat's feet.

Nat picked them up, then underhanded them through the open door.

'There's plenty of other guns around. If you come out with one of them, you'll force me to do something I don't want to do.'

With Spenser beside him, Nat edged backwards through the door and outside.

Drago lowered his hands and strode across the smithy to stand over Bell's prone form.

'I can deal with this one,' he said, tapping his foot against Bell's shoulder. 'If you want to take off after them.'

Creed narrowed his eyes. 'Can I trust you?'

'You can. We ain't got a problem any longer.' Drago held his hands wide. 'I like being deputized more than I like helping Bell.'

'Then I'm obliged.' Creed edged to the door and peered outside.

Spenser and Nat were still backing to their horses.

With his hands held chest high, Creed edged through the door and pressed his back to the smithy wall. He glanced at their former position.

Fairborn wasn't visible behind his previous cover.

While facing Nat and Spenser, Creed glanced from the corners of his eyes, then saw a shadow move behind a rock to his right. He circled away from it, keeping his gaze on Nat.

'Nat,' he shouted, 'this doesn't have to end this way for you.'

'Get back in the smithy,' Nat shouted, gesturing at Creed with his gun.

Creed paced to the side, crossing his legs over each other as he wandered sideways.

'I did what you asked. I ain't packing a gun. You got no reason to threaten me.'

The movement came again as the shadow flickered behind the rock. This time he was sure it was Fairborn.

Creed turned from the rock, but Spenser must have noticed his interest and swivelled at the hip, blasting a shot into the dirt beside the rock.

Creed broke into a run.

Twenty yards to his left, Fairborn leapt out from the rock. He rolled over a shoulder, lead from Spenser blasting over his tumbling form, and came up one knee.

But in a long dive, Creed leapt at Spenser and

grabbed him around the waist, bundling him to the ground.

Both men tumbled over each other, but Creed struggled until he was on top and pinned down Spenser's shoulders.

Cold steel pressed into his back.

'That's enough,' Nat muttered into his ear.

'Go on,' Creed muttered, straightening. 'Kill me.'

'We ain't lawmen-killers.'

Nat dragged Creed to his feet and swung him away from Spenser.

As Spenser stood, Fairborn rolled to his haunches and aimed his gun up at Nat, but Nat shook his head.

Fairborn glared at Nat a moment, then with an angry snort, threw his gun to the ground.

Creed backed five paces to stand alongside Fairborn and folded his arms.

'Yeah,' he muttered. 'You got principles. Except if you steal five thousand dollars, I won't use any principles when I track you down.'

With the barrel of his gun, Nat directed both lawmen to back from Fairborn's gun. Then he and Spenser edged backwards to their horses.

Nat blasted a single shot into the smithy beside the door, sending Drago to scurry back inside, then swung the bags from his shoulder. He unknotted the rope holding them, then dropped three bags and hoisted the smallest bag over his horse.

'What you doing?' Spenser muttered.

'Making it easier,' Nat said. 'The smaller bag has five thousand dollars in it.'

Spenser glanced at the bags. 'We ain't doing that.'

Nat narrowed his eyes. 'We don't need to leave the money somewhere for them to find later. We'll just leave it here.'

Spenser snorted. 'I didn't mean that. I mean they'll chase us down now that we've shot at a lawman. Things will be the same for us whether we've stolen five thousand or fifty thousand.'

'What?'

'You heard me. It was always coming to this, but now is the time to face it. We're disbanding the Ten Per Cent gang one way or the other after this job. I just reckon we disband it the proper way.'

Nat turned to face Spenser. 'We ain't doing that. We leave the bulk and take our recovery fee. We ain't outlaws.'

As both men glared at each, twenty yards away, Creed and Fairborn glanced at each other and shrugged.

Creed coughed. 'See the kind of man you have as a partner, Nat? You ain't like him.'

'Be quiet,' Spenser shouted. 'This is between me and Nat.'

'There's nothing between us,' Nat muttered. 'We have an agreement. We take ten per cent, nothing more.'

'And I ain't risking my life again for a measly ten per cent. I say it's time for a new agreement.' Spenser squared off to Nat and slammed his gun into its holster. He dangled his fingers beside the holster. 'From now on, we take it all.'

'We ain't gunslingers. We can't sort this argument out that way.'

'This is the only way we can sort this out.'

For long moments both men faced each other, then Nat slammed his gun in its holster and snorted.

'Suppose it was coming to this.'

Nat pulled down his hat to shield his eyes from the sun and as one, both men hunched down and edged their feet apart.

'Don't,' Fairborn shouted, but Creed slammed a hand over his mouth, silencing him.

Spenser flexed his hand and settled his stance with his fingers inches from his holster, his only movement the darting of his eyes as he appraised Nat's posture.

Nat was impassive as he glared deep into Spenser's eyes.

With matching gestures, both men pulled their hats a mite lower, then flexed their fingers.

For long moments, the only sound was the wind rustling through the corral fence, and the only movements were their jackets fluttering in the wind.

Then arms whirled as Spenser, then Nat, threw their hands to their holsters. In a smooth action Spenser's weapon cleared leather, but Nat's caught on the brim of his holster and using that fractional advantage Spenser fired first.

Nat folded and spun away, clutching his chest. He crashed to the ground and lay. His legs drew up. He writhed, then was still.

Spenser had already turned his gun on the two watching lawmen.

Fairborn snorted. 'The wrong man won.'

With the back of his hand, Spenser rubbed his brow.

'I reckon you're right. But stay back, lawmen.'

'We ain't coming any closer.' Creed snorted. 'But the man you killed was one of my deputies – even if temptation made him forget his duties for a moment. I'll track you down and you'll swing for that.'

Spenser shrugged. He dragged Nat's limp body to the horses, then pulled it on to the back of Nat's mount. While glaring at the lawmen, he swung the remaining three bags on to the back of his own horse and tethered the two animals together.

Then, with a last holler, he galloped from the smithy, pausing only to release and spook the lawmen's horses.

Creed watched the trail dust swirl as Spenser galloped into the plains and away from Lincoln, then patted Fairborn's shoulder. He couldn't stop his huge grin breaking out.

Drago and Turner edged outside to join them. Drago had slung the unconscious Bell over one broad shoulder.

With no pause to his grinning, Creed directed Turner to round up the horses.

'You ain't looking pleased, Fairborn,' Creed said.

'Spenser killed Nat. Despite his mistakes, Nat was a good man.'

'He was an outlaw.'

'He pushed the boundaries, but he was no outlaw. And you deputized him.' Fairborn sighed as he tipped back his hat. 'And he saved my life.'

'He made his choices.'

Fairborn swirled round to face Creed, his eyes blazing.

'But he died fighting over nothing.'

'Just like his kind always does.'

Drago joined them and hoisted Bell to the ground.

'But Nat died fighting over fifty thousand dollars,' he said. 'That ain't nothing.'

Creed chuckled. 'Nothing is all that was at stake.'

CHAPTER 20

Turner rounded up four horses and Drago tied and bundled the now conscious Bell on to one of them.

Then, with Bell tethered to Drago's mount, the group rode from the smithy, heading back to Lincoln, leaving a whistling Turner to return to his duties.

'You did a fine job as a deputy, Drago,' Creed said. 'Despite our disagreements before, you acted when you had to. You take to honesty better than you take to making underhand deals with the likes of Clayton Bell.'

'I reckon as you're right,' Drago said, nodding.

'If you ever want to work for me, I might be interested in your services. You could be an asset to Lincoln.'

Drago smiled. 'Is the pay better than being a wagon rider?'

'Nope,' Fairborn muttered. 'It's worse.'

'Obliged for the offer,' Drago murmured. He sighed. 'But if you want help tracking down Spenser, I'm willing to join you.'

Creed laughed. 'I ain't bothering. He can get

himself killed when he starts spending his money.'

'You have to get him.' Drago turned in the saddle. 'He's the biggest robber around these parts in years.'

'He ain't.' Creed tipped back his hat and treated Drago to his huge grin. 'He only stole the contents of my strongbox.'

'Yeah, the fifty thousand dollars you switched.'

'The false bottom does switch whatever was on the top to the bottom and whatever was on the bottom to the top.' Creed threw back his head and laughed long and hard. 'But that only happens if you trip the false bottom.'

'If you trip the false bottom,' Drago mused. He gulped. 'You didn't.'

'Nope. The counterfeit bills never left the false bottom of the strongbox and the real bills were always in your transportation carriage, until you abandoned them to chase after Bell's gang with me.'

Drago glanced over his shoulder back down the trail.

'But my men abandoned the carriage too. That means the cash is undefended.'

'It ain't. Fairborn saw to that.'

Fairborn sighed. 'Yeah, mine was just another sneaky act on a day of sneaky acts. The cash is safe. I buried it in a secure location.'

Drago blew out his cheeks, then yanked on Bell's rope and grinned.

'You hear that, Bell?'

Bell glared back at Creed, shaking his head.

'You shouldn't be proud of that, Sheriff,' he muttered. 'You're just as sneaky as me.'

Creed grinned. 'You're wrong. I'm sneakier.'

Then, aside from the occasional chuckle from Creed and Drago and the muttered oaths from Bell, the riders rode in silence to Lincoln.

But Fairborn's silence was a brooding one. The layers of duplicity he and Creed had just perpetrated bowed his back, and with every pace his guts grumbled some more and his brow knitted so hard he felt the flesh creak.

Four miles out of Lincoln, the train approached from behind them. They watched the engine rattle past, then hurried on to keep the train in sight.

Five minutes after the train trundled into Lincoln, they rode down the main road.

In the centre of the road, Mayor Lynch and a delegation of wagon riders were gesticulating widely as they shared an animated conversation. A circle of townsfolk was growing around them.

When the mayor saw the approaching lawmen, he pushed through the circle of onlookers and dashed towards them.

Creed licked his lips. 'I'm going to enjoy this.'

'Glad somebody is,' Fairborn muttered.

'Cheer up, Alan,' Creed said. 'We netted the Ten Per Cent gang and Clayton Bell in one go.'

'Only by ignoring everything the law stands for.'

'You idiot,' Mayor Lynch shouted, placing himself before Creed's horse with his hands on his hips. 'Bell raided you and stole fifty thousand dollars. Then he—'

'Stop there.' Creed dismounted and to his instructions, Drago dragged Bell from his horse. 'This is

Clayton Bell. He's under arrest and everyone else in his gang is dead.'

Mayor Lynch staggered back a pace, then looked Bell up and down.

'He doesn't look like much.'

'That's because he ain't.' Creed kicked Bell's rump, pushing him to his knees.

'Did you get back the fifty thousand too?'

'It's secure.'

Lynch whistled and rubbed his forehead. 'And the Ten Per Cent gang?'

'Either dead or misdirected.' Creed drew in a long breath of cool air. 'Perhaps the right word is disbanded.'

Mayor Lynch beamed. 'I always said you were a fine lawman and that you'd justify my faith in you.'

'Glad to hear it.' Creed puffed his chest. 'I reckon the townsfolk will call me the Ten Per Cent Sheriff for a while. And I'll be proud of it.'

Creed directed Drago to drag Bell to the cells in the sheriff's office, then turned to Fairborn.

'Get the money back, Alan. Then I reckon we've earned ourselves a celebratory drink.'

Fairborn glanced at the grinning mayor, then at his grinning boss, then at the hunched Clayton Bell disappearing into the sheriff's office. He glanced over his shoulder at the train.

'You and that toad, Jonah Eckstein, can get it. You complement each other.' Fairborn removed his badge from his pocket and threw it at Creed's feet. 'I quit.'

'But this is our greatest triumph.'

'It's yours. To catch Bell you lowered yourself to

the level of an outlaw.'

'The result is all that matters.'

'I don't agree. When you forget you're a lawman and double-deal, somebody pays the price. And in this case it was Nat McBain, a decent man.'

Creed shrugged. 'He made his choices.'

'And I've made mine. You once told me I had to decide how far I was prepared to go. Well, I've decided.' Fairborn glanced at the train. 'And the answer is Denver.'

Fairborn turned and strode across the road towards the station.

'Don't do this,' Creed shouted after him. 'You'll reconsider when you realize just what we've done here. We've sorted everything out.'

Fairborn stopped and turned. 'Hope you enjoy having everyone call you the Ten Per Cent Sheriff.'

Creed glared back, but Fairborn turned and strode to the station.

When he'd arrived in Lincoln two years ago, his only possessions were the clothes he wore. And now he revelled in leaving in the same state.

He boarded the train and sat in the seat at the back of the first passenger carriage. There, he could see down the main road.

From under a lowered hat, he watched Sheriff Creed collect and revel in the congratulations and back-slapping from all directions.

Drago emerged from the office and Creed patted him on the back. He glanced at the train, shook his head, then pinned Fairborn's badge on Drago's chest.

As both men strode to the bank, side by side, the train lurched to a start and edged from the station.

Just as the main road disappeared from Fairborn's view, Creed charged from the bank, his face bright red and his arms wheeling.

On the train, Fairborn leaned back in his seat, smiling. He swung his legs on to the opposite seat and pulled his hat low.

In a copse, ten miles out of Lincoln, a lone man sat astride his horse. The man was plump, short and balding. A rifle lay across his lap.

A bulging saddlebag lay over the back of his horse. On the ground before him, two more bulging saddlebags lay.

He watched two riders trot towards him, one fair-haired, the other darker. The two riders slowed to a halt.

With a steady movement, the fair-haired rider swung his Peacemaker from its holster, but kept it held across his chest as the dark-haired man swung down from his horse and edged to the saddlebags. He threw one open and looked up, smiling, then tipped his hat.

'Time we called an end to our agreement and made our own way,' he said.

The short man nodded and backed his horse.

'It is.'

'Where you heading?'

'I'm not looking to cause you offence, but I'm not answering that. Likewise, I'm not interested in your plans.'

'Understood. And believe me when I say that Nat and me won't look for you.' Spenser swung the first saddlebag on to his shoulder and grabbed the second. 'There's more than enough here without us getting greedy.'

'Then we think the same way.'

Spenser swung the first saddlebag on to the back of Nat's horse, then swung the second on to his horse.

Nat edged forward and tipped his hat. 'I'll say goodbye, Jonah. We've pretty much removed everyone that could have come after us, but that still leaves Sheriff Creed and we reckon he'll come looking for you first. He's sure to realize you were the only one who knew where Fairborn buried the shipment.'

'I reckon that sheriff isn't as stupid as you think. He'll figure the rest out before too long and he'll come looking for you too.'

'Perhaps.' Nat edged his jacket open and glanced down at his clean shirt. 'But he kind of has the idea that I'm dead and that he fooled Spenser. He'll think of you first.'

Jonah nodded. 'I thank you for your advice. But I'll leave you now. I have my fifteen thousand dollars to enjoy.'

Spenser paused beside his horse and narrowed his eyes.

'Fifteen thousand dollars each ain't what we expected. Fifty thousand dollars was supposed to be in the shipment.'

Jonah chuckled. 'Sorry, but I figured that we were rich enough now to enjoy winding up Creed even more.'

Spenser glared back, but Nat matched Jonah's chuckle.

'That was a fine idea.'

'What idea?' Spenser asked as he mounted his horse, but Nat shook his head and backed his horse from the copse.

Matching Nat's movements, Jonah backed his horse. Then, when he was fifty yards away, he shook the reins and hurtled away in a cloud of dust.

Nat watched him leave, then nodded to Spenser. In a simultaneous shaking of the reins, the two men hurtled away in the opposite direction.

Spenser drew his horse alongside Nat's horse.

'You going to tell me what was so funny about us not getting all of the fifty thousand?'

'Do the math. Fifteen thousand for three men means he left five thousand for Creed to find.'

Spenser bit his lip as he calculated, then allowed himself a smile.

'I see what you mean. That was the Ten Per Cent gang's last job – and this time, we left ten per cent.'

Five minutes out of Lincoln, the conductor sauntered into Fairborn's carriage.

'Ticket,' he murmured when he reached Fairborn.

'Denver,' Fairborn said, tipping back his hat. 'One way.'

The conductor peeled off a ticket and took Fairborn's money, then narrowed his eyes.

'You not planning on returning then, Deputy Fairborn?'

'Nope. And I ain't a deputy no more.'

'Pity, from what I hear, you did a good job back in Lincoln.'

'Thanks for your support.' Fairborn glanced at the ticket, then slipped it into his pocket. 'But it's time to move on.'

'What you planning to do in Denver?'

'A wagon rider might be the right job for me. The banks might appreciate having an honest man guarding their cash shipments.'

'I wish you luck,' the conductor said and moved on to the next passenger.

For long moments, Fairborn stared through the window, watching the barren plains pass by. Then he swung his legs down to the floor.

From under his seat, he removed the shovel that he'd used to bury his own stash of forged cash and threw it on to the seat opposite. Then he reached under that seat, extracted four bulging bags, and placed them on the seat between himself and the train wall.

'I don't need luck,' Fairborn said to himself as he patted the bags. 'I reckon the safe delivery of fifty thousand dollars will make a mighty powerful statement.'